THE PRINCE'S FAKE FIANCÉE

LEAH ASHTON

MILLS & BOON

First published in Great Britain 2017
by Mills & Boon, an imprint of HarperCollins*Publishers*
1 London Bridge Street, London, SE1 9GF

Large Print edition 2018

© 2017 Leah Ashton

ISBN: 978-0-263-07372-0

MIX
Paper from
responsible sources
FSC® C007454

This book is produced from independently certified
FSC™ paper to ensure responsible forest management.
For more information visit www.harpercollins.co.uk/green.

Printed and bound in Great Britain
by CPI Group (UK) Ltd, Croydon, CR0 4YY

For my grandmother, Marica,
who inspired this story.

Not just with her homeland of Vela Luka,
but also with her sixty-five-year romance
with Rafé, which was the kind of love that
dreams and romance novels are made of.

Thank you for all your help with this book.

Thank you also for your food, your garden
and all your love.

Hvala, Nana.

CHAPTER ONE

JASMINE GALLAGHER SAT in the back seat of a sleek, dark sedan, silently observing the passing countryside behind windows tinted almost black.

The road hugged the very edge of the island of Vela Ada, almost touching the perfect blue of the Adriatic Sea. It was late afternoon, and the ocean glittered beneath the glorious summer sun, the azure surface interrupted only by the occasional tall-masted boat with sails in blinding white.

Jasmine's car was the third of three identical vehicles. Leading the small convoy were two of Jas's team: Scott—who was ex-Special Forces— and Heather—who, like Jas, was ex-Australian National Police. Next in line was what was called the 'principal's' car—the person that Gallagher Personal Protection Services had been tasked with protecting. In Jas's career she had provided close personal protection services—what most people outside the industry would call a 'bodyguard'—to a wide range of people: prime ministers, ambassadors, religious leaders, CEOs, celebrities—but this job was a first for her, and a first for her company.

From today—and for the next three months—she was looking after a prince.

Jasmine smiled. *Royalty.*

This was the opportunity of a lifetime for a girl who'd grown up in public housing on the outskirts of Canberra. And further confirmation that those naysayers who told her a woman couldn't be the face of a protection services company were clueless.

Not that Jasmine had ever doubted herself.

The dense forest that faced the harbour thinned as the convoy approached the city. At a predetermined landmark—a distinctive cast-iron lamp just over a kilometre from the palace—Jas picked up her phone.

'We're approaching,' she said.

As Jasmine ended the call the woman seated beside her shifted in her seat.

'Can you quiz me again?' she asked, her voice just slightly high pitched. Jas met the gaze of their driver, Simon—a retired SAS Commando—in the rear-view mirror, and knew he was smiling. Felicity had been asking for help with her script and backstory ever since they'd picked her up from

Dubrovnik airport, and then over the several hours it had taken to drive and then ferry to Vela Ada.

'You've got this,' Jasmine reassured her. 'But we can run through it one more time if you like.'

Felicity nodded. 'Thank you. I know I'm being ridiculous. I *know*, I know this, it's just…' she paused, pushing her long, perfectly curled blonde hair behind her ears '…this isn't a normal acting job, is it? And Marko… I mean, you've met him, right? *Prince Marko…?* He's pretty distracting.'

Jasmine laughed. 'I can't say I personally feel that way, but guess I can imagine why that would be.'

If you were the type to find tall, dark, broad-shouldered Mediterranean princes distracting. Which Jasmine was not. She couldn't afford to be distracted by something as irrelevant as attractiveness in her job.

'Oh, come *on*,' Felicity said, narrowing her eyes. 'You're not that much older than me, and you're not dead, so don't pretend you haven't noticed he's totally hot. And that *accent*. Honestly, he could read a dictionary and make it sound sexy. Why don't Aussie guys sound like that?'

She flopped back into her leather seat, and now Simon—also Australian—was quietly laughing as the car slowed to a crawl to navigate the narrow cobblestone streets of the city.

'So, I met Marko in Rome six months ago, during a break, while he completed a secondment with the Italian Army and while I was on holiday. It was *terrifically* romantic...'

Jasmine nodded as Felicity spoke. Jasmine had, of course, been briefed on this rather unusual arrangement—although she didn't know every detail that Felicity was running through now. But she wasn't worried—Felicity was whip-smart, and very well prepared. Ivan—the Prince's valet—had told her of Felicity's exceptional improvisation skills as well, so she was clearly an excellent choice. Plus she certainly looked the part—even now, just slightly anxious, the blonde woman oozed class and polish.

The perfect princess. Or rather, princess-to-be.

'And he took me on a picnic to propose—at the Pavlovic Estate.' Felicity paused. 'I mean, can you imagine if that actually happened? If Prince Marko actually proposed to me for real?' She sighed, and closed her eyes as if imagining the moment herself. '*Princess* Felicity!' She shrugged. 'Oh, well, best enjoy it while it lasts. And do my best to make it believable that Europe's most notorious playboy would *actually* settle down.'

'You've got this,' Jas repeated, but then added, more seriously, 'But remember, your engagement might be fake, but no one else knows that. Your security is real. We don't have any intel that suggests Prince Marko is under threat, but if he was—to any potential bad guys, you *are* his fiancée, and you *will* be a princess. So it's important for your own safety that you follow my instructions tonight, and over the next few months. Okay?'

Felicity nodded. 'Of course,' she said.

Jas watched as Felicity straightened her shoulders and adjusted her expression. No longer did even a hint of the actress remain—she was every inch the mysterious fiancée who Marko would be introducing to Vela Ada at tonight's ball.

The car slid to a stop at the security checkpoint at the palace gate.

Now in range, Jas activated her earpiece. 'We're here.'

Marko sank back into the linen fabric of his couch, and rubbed his temples.

He had a cracking headache, right on top of the fuzzy cloak of fatigue he'd been wearing all week.

Across from him, in separate plush single armchairs, sat his valet, and the head of his new security detail—Jasmine Gallagher. Beyond that pair was a massive window, framed with heavy brocade curtains and so sparkling clean as to appear invisible. Through that—if he looked—he could see the entire east side of the island—a stunning view but also rather useful when the palace had also played the role of military lookout several centuries ago. Built at the island's highest point, Palace Vela Ada had three-hundred-and-sixty-degree views of the tiny island nation—of its single undulating city of red-roofed stone houses, of the tiny towns dotted amongst the vineyards and market gardens that spoke of its rich agricultural industry, and of the boats and yachts that bobbed in the ocean and brought in as many tourist dollars now as the fish.

But Marko wasn't looking at the view, because he didn't really want to be here at all.

He wanted to be back in Italy, he wanted to be the man who had just been promoted to Pukovnik—Lieutenant Colonel—and who had been thrilled at his progress in strengthening ties between the minuscule Vela Adian army and their allies in neighbouring Croatia and Italy. He also wanted to be the man who—much of the time—managed to ignore the reality of being a prince.

Sure, he was treated differently in the army—but it was subtle, now, after years of his adamant refusal to be coddled and protected or elevated to a rank he hadn't earned. He'd earned the respect of his peers through hard work and later through tours of duty. He was Lieutenant Colonel Marko Pavlovic first; *Prince* Marko only really made an appearance at official royal events, and even that was rare, as his brother—King Lukas—seriously had that all in hand.

It was the greatest stroke of luck that Lukas had been born two years before Marko, rather than the other way around, as Lukas had been the perfect king-in-training since birth. He was everything a king should be, leading Vela Ada through the last few years of political unrest as the Vela Adian parliament had been rocked by scandal and corruption.

Now the dust had—almost—settled, but then Lukas had been diagnosed with cancer.

In the week since Lukas had called him, Marko had been in a fog. He was labelling it fatigue, but it was different from that, really. More a heavy weight of uncertainty and fear.

Lukas—and the royal doctor—had assured Marko and the royal family that Lukas's form of cancer was highly treatable, and that his prospects of making a full recovery were extremely good. He'd also gone to great lengths to stress that Lukas's cancer was unrelated to the cancer that had killed their father, the late King Josip.

But Marko couldn't imagine life without his brother. They might be as different as night and day, but there was no one on this planet Marko respected more than Lukas. Nobody.

Marko couldn't say for sure that was how Lukas felt about *him*—but that didn't really matter. Especially not now.

'I need you to step up for me, Marko,' Lukas had said. 'The island can't cope with any more turmoil. My people need to feel safe, they need to trust our government and know that we—the heads of state—are in control and incorruptible. You need to be—for once in your life—respectful of your position. Respectful of your responsibilities. You can't run away any longer.'

Marko had bristled—despite his concern for Lukas he was unable to leave that comment unchallenged. 'No one would ever dare question my commitment to our military,' he'd said, his tone hard-edged.

'Your commitment to training all over the world, you mean?' Lukas had said. 'Italy, Australia, the US, France...'

His brother had sighed.

'Look, I'm incredibly proud of what you've

achieved in your career, and what you've done for our defence alliances—but would it have killed you to spend a bit more time in Vela Ada? To actually be visible to your people? To support them in a way that is tangible to them? Especially over the past few years? Instead, all they see of you is photos in glossy magazines. What was the last article on you? Something about top ten royals in their swimwear... I mean, well done on being number one and all...' Lukas's tone had been desert dry '...but honestly—you were with a different woman in every single photo. How do you think that looks to our people?'

'It's none of their business,' Marko said firmly.

'That's the point,' Lukas had said—for the first time sounding as tired and unwell as he really was. 'You're a prince. Their Prince. It is their business that you'd rather spend your time anywhere but here and with a different woman every week.'

The phone had been silent for long moments.

'This isn't going to work, is it?' said Lukas. 'I know you're capable of caretaking my role, but perception is the problem. If people don't believe in you, they won't feel safe. And I can't have that. We've worked too hard to prosecute Senator Božić and his allies and rid Vela Ada of this scourge. Look, I know the label's not entirely accurate, but

will they believe in the Playboy Prince? Maybe I can still be active, in between treatments. Try and downplay my illness, and don't mention it's cancer...'

His brother was talking faster and faster.

'Stop,' Marko said. 'I'm not the Playboy Prince. Not any more.' He'd paused, trying to work out what he could say to reassure his brother. He hated hearing his usually impeccably calm and measured brother so anxious. He also hated— as he'd always hated—the way his personal life was even relevant to Vela Adians—and that his brother bought into it too. Surely his years of military service outweighed a selection of photos of him with bikini-clad women? But this wasn't the time for that argument. 'I'm engaged,' he blurted out the moment the idea even partially formed in his brain. 'I wanted to tell you in person. So you needn't worry. The Playboy Prince is no more.'

'Really?' Lukas had been stunned. 'That's perfect. I mean—congratulations!'

'Thank you,' Marko had said, his lips quirking upwards.

'Who is she? I didn't know you were dating anyone.'

Because, of course, he hadn't been. Marko searched his mind and the room for some titbit about this mystery woman he could share with his brother. On the wall of the small hotel room was an aged map of the world, and his gaze fell to the right-hand corner. 'She's Australian,' he said, thinking fast. 'I met her six months ago. How about she comes with me to Vela Ada, next week, so you can meet her?'

'Yes—' Lukas had said, sounding like himself again. 'I'll announce my illness this week and then have a ball a few days later to reassure everyone I'm not about to keel over, and to reposition you as a stable, responsible, engaged caretaker head of state. I like it.'

'A ball, Lukas? That's really not my thing—'

'It is for the next three months, Marko. You'd better get used to it.'

Marko's gaze slid from the view to the people before him. Ivan sat neatly in his ever-present pin-striped suit, listening intently and studiously taking notes. Beside him, Jasmine—also in a suit—was talking of safe rooms, escape routes and tonight's schedule.

'Your Highness,' she said, her tone suddenly steelier. 'This is important. I appreciate that Ivan will probably brief you again later, but for your safety—and for the safety of my team and everyone in the palace—you need to pay attention.'

Now his gaze sharpened. Before he'd simply been aware that a woman in a jet-black pant-suit sat across from him, but she was right—he hadn't been paying attention. He hadn't even really looked at her. This week had been such a blur of bad news, upturning his life and coordinating his impulsive 'fiancée' lie, that he'd simply approved the appointment of Gallagher Personal Protection Services based on the recommendation of Palace Security and thought little more about the woman who headed the company.

Now he properly considered her.

She was quite tall—obvious even when seated thanks to her long, crossed legs and the fact that her shoulders sat almost level with Ivan's. Her hair was dark, and tied back sleekly from her pale skin, with not one stray strand obscuring the curved line of her cheeks and straight edge of her jaw. Right now, that jaw was firm as she studied him with intense brown eyes.

No, hazel eyes, he corrected as he continued to just look at her, and as the sun that streamed through the window highlighted the flecks of gold in her gaze.

She had great eyes, he realised—large and framed with thick lashes and neat eyebrows as black as her hair. And sharp—as if she missed nothing.

Which would come handy in her job, he supposed.

She hadn't missed his perusal. He felt her intent gaze as his continued to track its way down her narrow, ski-slope-shaped nose—with the slightest upturned tip. It was a nose that probably veered closer towards large than small—and it sat above lips that were neither large nor small. Pink though, and glossy.

Her chin—like her jaw—was firm. A stubborn chin, most likely—but again, this was probably a trait useful in her profession.

Overall, he'd say she was pretty. Certainly pretty enough that in any other week of his life he would've noticed that fact immediately. But he barely remembered what his fake fiancée looked like, and he'd met with her via video conference and face to face nearly a dozen times this week.

His gaze slid back up to hers. Actually, her eyes were definitely more than pretty…beautiful, really—

'Your Highness, may I assume that you also spend this much time documenting the appearance of your male security personnel?'

Marko blinked. Jasmine's eyes were hard.

'My apologies—' he began.

'My gender is irrelevant, Your Highness. And I have certainly not been employed for you to look at.'

'No—of course not—'

Marko couldn't remember the last time he'd felt so flustered. He'd say most people who knew him would assume he never was.

'But if we can agree that I'm not to be either ignored, or ogled, from now on, I think we can continue with my briefing.'

Marko nodded, not just a little ashamed of his behaviour. She was absolutely right—he'd had a terrible week, but it didn't excuse what he'd just done.

What was wrong with him?

He needed to pull himself together. He needed to commit to this—to this stupid plan of his—with everything he had.

He needed to do this for Lukas.

And for Vela Ada.

'I sincerely apologise, Ms Gallagher,' Marko said, again meeting her gaze squarely. 'I assure you it won't happen again.'

She raised an eyebrow, but then she nodded. A neat, controlled movement—like all her movements, he suspected.

He didn't like that she clearly didn't believe him. Did Jasmine think he was the Playboy Prince, too? That he was some frivolous, useless heartbreaker who'd abandoned his country and left his brother to deal with all that royalty bother while he flitted around the world enjoying himself?

Probably.

And he wouldn't be able to talk her around, especially after that rather woeful first impression.

He didn't bother to analyse why it mattered what the head of his protection team thought of him—he knew, instinctively, it wouldn't make any difference to the quality of service that Jasmine would provide.

But it did matter.

Maybe because he genuinely *wasn't* the man who—as Jasmine had said—*ogled* his employees. Or maybe it was because if he wanted all of Vela Ada to respect him, he needed to start with the people standing around him.

Or maybe it was just because Jasmine Gallagher had remarkable golden eyes.

CHAPTER TWO

AFTER THE BRIEFING, Jasmine excused herself to escape to her room.

She nodded at Simon in the hallway, stationed outside Felicity's suite, but didn't meet his gaze. The blush she'd somehow suppressed throughout Marko's…assessment? Inventory? She didn't know how to describe it, but her blush was working its way up her neck at a rate of knots. She needed to get to her room before anyone noticed.

Because Jas Gallagher *did not* blush.

Fortunately, her room was adjacent to Felicity's, and so only a few doors down from Prince Marko's. Safe inside, she flopped onto her bed and stared at the ceiling. At the ornately painted ceiling rose and small glittering chandelier, to be specific, because her room was as sumptuous as the Prince's suite. Just significantly smaller.

Although—in the Pavlovic Palace—small was certainly relative. It was actually about the size of her two-bedroom flat back in Canberra.

Jas squeezed her eyes shut.

Palace. Royalty, she reminded herself.

This job was important. Significant, even. It was highly unusual for an external company to provide personal protection services to immediate members of any royal family. Usually such services for dignitaries would be provided by a country's government—either the royal's own government, or, if visiting another nation, by that nation's own police. When she'd been with the Australian National Police she'd often worked on the shoulder of ambassadors, presidents and prime ministers—simply because laws in Australia prevented visiting protection teams from carrying firearms.

This opportunity—possible only because of the lack of suitably qualified Vela Adian protection personnel, and the expediency that protection services were required—was as rare as it got.

So biting off the head of said actual royal was probably not advisable.

Although obviously she was always going to say something. She would never let a client ignore her like that—and then *stare* at her like that—without comment. It wasn't acceptable behaviour. Personal protection didn't work without respect—of her, of her team, of her directions. It was non-negotiable.

But still—had she had to draw attention to the

fact she was a woman? It was something she—as she'd told the Prince—considered irrelevant. And hence, it was not a topic she ever engaged in.

Despite contrary advice, she'd always been very visible as the head of her company. There were no surprises to anyone who hired Gallagher Personal Protection Services that the person in charge was a woman. It was a self-selecting strategy—if some-one was too closed minded to realise that Galla-gher was awesome at what it did, just because she didn't have broad shoulders and a… Well, then that was definitely their issue. Not hers.

She wasn't about to defend or justify or do any-thing else to explain herself, because of course to tell anyone that being female *wasn't* an issue *be-cause* of x, y and z implied that she entertained their concerns. And she did not.

Actions spoke louder than words. She'd learnt that the hard way after—

Jas dug her fingernails into her palms. *No.* It had been months since she'd thought about what had happened, and she wasn't about to start now. What mattered now was she hated that she'd brought up her gender to the Prince. Why would she do that?

Because he'd made her feel so female...

Ugh.

What was it about Prince Marko? Despite what

she'd told Felicity, she *had* noticed how unbelievably gorgeous he was the few brief times they'd met. Because he was gorgeous in person in a way that was surprising, and almost *overwhelming*, despite her being familiar with his looks because... well, if you'd ever picked up a women's magazine, anywhere in the world, you'd heard of the Playboy Prince.

In person, his looks were just more intense: he was taller, broader, and his blue eyes more piercing than she ever could've imagined.

And despite looking like a man who'd received upsetting news about his brother—with the olive skin of his jaw dusted with stubble, his eyes tinged red, and the occasional grey hair in his army buzz-cut dark hair—such dishevelment just made him even more appealing to her: raw, and real.

And for some reason that real prince—after barely glancing at her for almost the entirety of their business arrangement—had decided to stare at her today.

And if she'd thought his looks intense before—being on the receiving end of his concentrated attention was something else entirely.

The instant he'd really looked at her, her blood had run hot and her belly had heated. She'd sat perfectly still as his eyes had travelled across her face—and she was certain she'd briefly stopped breathing as he'd caught her gaze. As she'd begun to feel herself get lost within it...

But then he'd moved on: his gaze like a touch along her nose, her bare lips, and her skin that seemed so pale amongst Mediterranean complexions.

How long had he stared at her?

It had felt like an age—but maybe it was no time at all?

Maybe—and, God, she cringed at her choice of words now—it hadn't been an *ogle* at all?

It would make more sense if it hadn't been, really. She knew she wasn't unattractive, but she was no Felicity. Her nose was a little too big, her hair nondescript and her figure was more athletic than voluptuous.

But she didn't really believe that. He might not have planned to do it—but she knew when a man was checking her out.

Jas's eyes snapped open, and she studied the way the setting sun reflected off the crystal beads of the chandelier above her.

Not that it mattered if Marko *had* checked her out.

What mattered was that she'd spoken without thinking first. She could've made her point in a myriad other ways without drawing attention to the two things she wanted Prince Marko to forget about completely: that she was a woman, and that he'd been appreciating that fact.

A sharp knock on her door snapped Jas out of her self-recrimination.

She sat up, and straightened her shoulders.

She was being ridiculous. What was done was done.

From now on, she would simply revert to being as impeccably professional as she always—usually—was.

Besides, she seriously doubted that the Prince was likely to check her out again—today was surely a blip?—which would make things easier.

Another insistent knock on her door, and Jas was on her feet. A moment later, she opened the door. It was Simon, and Jas blinked, surprised. It was several hours before they would be accompanying Marko and Felicity to the ball.

Simon spoke in a low, urgent tone. 'We have a problem.'

Felicity sat curled up in a brocade wingback chair beside her room's windows—but she'd closed the heavy curtains and blocked the setting sun. The room was lit only by a single bedside lamp, its glow revealing Felicity's evening gown, laid across the bed in a cascade of emerald silk.

'I'm so sorry,' Felicity said brokenly, and Jas ran to her side, dropping to her knees beside the chair.

'Don't be,' she said, gripping the other woman's hand. 'Of course you need to go home.'

Felicity had just received news that her mother and father had been hospitalised with serious injuries following a terrible car accident. Fortunately neither parent was in a critical condition, but there was no question that Felicity needed to be back in Australia to support her family right now—and not in Vela Ada.

'What is Marko going to do, though? He needs a fiancée. I feel terrible, I—'

'Don't stress about it. You just worry about getting home. Can I help pack your things for you?'

Felicity nodded as Jas got back to her feet.

'I'm sure the Prince will sort something out—' Jas began.

'I certainly will,' a deep voice said from behind her. Jas turned to see Ivan and Marko framed in the doorway.

'Your car is ready to take you to the airport,' he said as he approached Felicity. He also dropped to his haunches so he was at Felicity's level. 'I'm sincerely sorry to hear about your parents' accident. I'll make sure you get home as quickly as possible.'

He stood, and offered his hand to help Felicity up. The blonde woman took it gratefully, and then headed for the door.

'My things—' she began.

'I've got it under control,' Jas reassured her. 'I'll get it all sorted and send it down to the car.'

And then Felicity—and Ivan—were gone.

Somehow, Jas had ended up alone in a room with Prince Marko.

She sent him a tight smile, assuming he'd leave in a moment, and busied herself with locating Felicity's suitcase.

She jumped when he spoke just as she opened one of the built-in cupboards. It seemed he hadn't, in fact, gone anywhere.

'This is not ideal.'

Jas couldn't help but grin at that understatement. She knew exactly how much planning had gone into tonight.

'I assumed you would just announce that your fiancée had a family emergency,' Jas said. It was, after all, the only option he had.

Suitcase found, Jas grabbed it and turned—to find the Prince sitting on the edge of Felicity's expansive bed.

The image of Prince Marko in—well, *on*—a bed had her momentarily transfixed.

It was the most innocent of poses—he literally just sat on it, fully clothed in suit trousers, and a crisp white shirt, unbuttoned at the neck.

He wasn't even looking at Jas, his attention, instead, on the dress that lay beside him. The fingers of one hand were absently twisting a fold of the delicate fabric.

And yet being alone in a room with the only man she could remember ever having…*unsettled* her—*distracted* her—the way he had just by *looking* at her was disconcerting.

Despite her personal pep talk only minutes ago, Jas certainly felt less than purely professional right now. She was spending far too long admiring how the breadth of his shoulders was emphasised by the cut of his shirt, and how its slim fit and the musculature it skimmed reminded Jas of his military day job. Again, she had the sense of something raw and hard in Prince Marko, a world away from the perfect Playboy Prince that she had imagined.

'That won't work,' the Prince said, now looking at Jasmine.

The intensity of his gaze—or maybe that was just how he looked at everybody—once again knocked Jas off balance. She looked down, reminding herself of the empty suitcase in her hands, which she was gripping so hard her knuckles had turned white.

'Oh?' Jasmine said, not really following—instead refocusing her attention on her task. She needed to get this bag packed for Felicity, not worry about princes and beds.

'No,' said Marko, 'I need a tangible princess-to-be, someone for the people of Vela Ada to fall in love with. Unfortunately I don't have what my brother has, that innate—'

'Kingliness?' Jas prompted as she skirted the end of the bed to lay the suitcase beside the evening gown, and as far from Marko as she could manage. She had considered laying it on one of the couches, or on the floor, instead—before she'd told herself she was again being ridiculous.

Marko laughed out loud, the sound deep and rich and filling the room.

Jas's head jerked upwards as she only belatedly realised what she'd actually said. *What was it about this man that made her speak before she thought?* 'Oh, gosh, I'm sorry, that was a stupid thing for me to say—'

But he shook his head. 'No,' he said. 'It's perfect. It's exactly why I'm doing this. Vela Ada needs a king right now—but as Lukas isn't available, it's on me. But I'm not—how did you put it?—*kingly* enough and I know it. Put me in a war zone and I know what I'm doing. Put me in front of the population of Vela Ada…and I hate it. I hate the scrutiny of my personal life. I hate how carefully every word and sentence needs to be constructed. I hate balls and cutting ribbons at the opening of things and having to always be gracious and polite and shake everybody's hand…and everyone knows it.' Marko rubbed his temples, his gaze again on the fabric of the dress. 'No one's going to believe I suddenly have all this *kingliness* in me, unless they believe I've actually changed. That I'm no longer the Playboy Prince.'

And that was why he needed an actual, real-life, in-person fiancée.

She got that now. But…

'Why are you telling me this?' she asked, confused. Her hands had stilled on the zip of the suitcase, packing once again forgotten.

He didn't know her. Why would he reveal so much personal stuff to the head of his security detail? She and her team had only known enough of Marko's plan to allow them to protect the Prince and Felicity effectively. Nothing more.

She watched as Marko pushed himself to his feet and then carefully lifted the emerald dress so that it hung from his fingertips before him. It was a stunning dress, with delicate cap sleeves, a sweetheart neckline, and a slim gold belt at the waist. Beneath that, it fell in a full skirt to the floor, in waves of heavy, shimmering fabric.

A crazy possibility—the *craziest* possibility—tickled at the edge of Jas's subconscious.

'Do you think this would fit you?' Prince Marko asked.

'Pardon me?'

Jasmine's eyes were wide in the shadowy lamplight.

But there was no need for Marko to spell it out—he knew Jasmine understood what he'd meant.

'It's the obvious solution,' he said. It had been obvious to him the moment he'd walked into Felicity's room and seen Jasmine there. 'I need a fiancée *tonight* and no offence to Ivan, but you're the only one who knows about any of this who will look good in this dress.'

He gave the dress a little shake for emphasis.

'I'm not an actress, Your Highness,' Jasmine said carefully, her shocked expression now completely erased. Instead she looked very calm, as if she intended to talk him out of this using common sense.

Of course, this whole idea was nonsensical right

from the beginning—Marko knew that. But his impulsiveness was only equalled by his stubbornness—and his commitment to supporting his brother through his illness.

'That doesn't matter,' Marko said patiently. 'You'll be expected to be a little nervous at your first public event—it will be endearing. And, please, call me Marko.'

Jasmine shook her head, ignoring him. 'Haven't you shown a photo of Felicity to your brother? Told people she's blonde? And even today—we arrived in daylight and I'm sure a few palace staff would've seen her?'

Marko shrugged. 'She was my guest. Or your guest, even—easily explained. And fortunately I've told my brother very little. I don't like lying to him.'

Jasmine raised her eyebrows at that contradiction, but Marko wasn't about to explain. It was true though, he had told Lukas very little—partly for the reason he'd told Jasmine, but also because the week had been such a blur. Ivan had become responsible for the details.

'This is ridiculous. I'm a bodyguard, not a princess. No one's going to believe it.'

'Of course they will,' Marko said firmly. 'If I introduce you as my fiancée, then you're my fiancée.'

Jasmine was looking down again, fiddling rest-lessly with the zip of the suitcase. 'But,' she said. And now she met his gaze, back to the no-non-sense Jasmine he was already familiar with. 'Let's face it, I don't look anything like one of your girl-friends.'

'I'm not having a discussion about the appear-ance of the women you, or anyone else, thinks I date, Jasmine.' He knew there was an edge to his tone, but it was unavoidable. 'All I will say is that I enjoy the company of many types of women. I can see nothing unbelievable about me dating you.'

He was surprised to see Jasmine's lips quirk up-wards. 'Many types...' she repeated.

Marko narrowed his eyes. 'Yes, many,' he agreed. 'I like the company of women. I'm not going to apologise for it.'

Not nearly as many women as Jasmine, or ev-eryone else, seemed to think. But he wasn't about to explain himself to her.

He could see Jasmine thinking. 'Why not make up a reason why your fiancée is absent tonight, and then find a new actress? You found Felicity quickly. I'm sure you can do it again.'

Marko shook his head. 'No. Tonight is impor-tant. Vela Ada just found out their King is seriously ill. Tonight is the night they need to meet my new fiancée.'

Jasmine chewed her lip, and he knew she was scrambling for a reason to get out of this. 'And this fiancée would be *me*. Jasmine Gallagher, right? No fake name?'

Marko nodded. The press would be onto this—as with Felicity, it would've been too high risk to create a false identity, with the consequences of being found out catastrophic. So, it was the relationship that was fake, nothing more.

'So—assuming everyone *does* believe that I am princess material, it'll mean that my friends and family will think I've been hiding this from them for six months.'

'You can say it was at my request,' he said. 'They'll understand.'

'But that would be a *lie*,' Jasmine said. 'I would be lying, not only to everyone in Vela Ada, but to everyone I know.'

'Yes,' Marko agreed. 'Unfortunately that would be the case.'

Jasmine gave a little huff of frustration. 'That's not a small thing.'

'It's not,' he acknowledged. 'But for me, for the King, and for Vela Ada, the benefits far outweigh a small untruth.'

Jasmine raised an eyebrow. 'And for me?'

'You get to be a princess for a while?' he said, a little hopefully.

'Try again,' she said, crossing her arms.

'I'll triple the fee I'm paying you for protection services.'

He watched as her mouth dropped open.

But quick as a flash her lips were arranged in a straight line again. 'I'd argue that doing this could be detrimental to my business.'

'Yet you've been seeing me for six months with no impact on the quality of services you provide.'

Again, Jasmine raised an eyebrow. 'Ha-ha,' she said, as flat as a pancake.

'I have contacts,' Marko said—more seriously now. 'Through the military, and through diplomatic relationships. I promise you that your company will have more work at the end of this, not less.'

She nodded. 'But what about me, personally? I love what I do, not just managing my company. Who will want a princess as their bodyguard?'

'Well,' he said practically, 'in three months' time, you *won't* be a princess. And three months after that, everyone would've forgotten who you are.'

'Ouch,' she said.

He shrugged. 'It's true. And to help that along,

I'll make sure to date someone famous on the rebound. Draw the attention away from you.'

Her expression was sceptical. 'So you'll enter into *another* fake relationship after this one?'

Marko grinned. 'No. I'll just ask a good friend of mine who I date occasionally if she'd mind being photographed with me. She has a film out later this year, so I'm sure she won't mind. It's never been her that's been concerned about discretion.'

'You casually date a *movie star*?' But she held up her hand before he could respond. 'No, wait. Of *course* you do. You're a prince. Royalty. Celebrities. They go together. Can't you see that I don't fit into your world?'

'Right now, all that I really care about is if you'll fit into this dress.'

Jasmine's gaze dropped to the dress he still held.

Long moments passed as he watched Jasmine make her decision—and for the first time he seriously considered what he'd do if she said no.

And honestly, why wouldn't she say no? All of her concerns were valid, except, of course, her belief that a relationship between them was unbelievable.

He'd thought her pretty before, during the briefing. He found her even more attractive now—in the soft, warm lamplight. She was right—she probably *wasn't* exactly his type, in that she was more quietly pretty. Not like Felicity, who everyone noticed the moment she stepped into a room. But Jasmine…he liked how she looked at him so directly, and he really liked how she'd challenged him during the briefing, and how she'd questioned him now. She treated him like an equal—exactly as she should, but how so very few people did. It was, again, one of the many things about his royal title that sat so uncomfortably on his shoulders. He wasn't special simply due to the fortune of his birth. He didn't ask, or expect, to be treated differently from anybody else.

'Yes,' Jasmine said, suddenly. 'I'll do it.'

Marko's gaze caught hers as he exhaled in relief. '*Hvala*…thank you,' he said. 'You have no idea how much this means to me.'

She smiled, and he saw understanding in those lovely hazel eyes. 'Oh,' she said. 'I think I do.'

CHAPTER THREE

THE DRESS DIDN'T FIT.

Well, more accurately, it didn't fit *yet*.

Jas sat on the closed lid of the toilet within her—literally—palatial bathroom, having quickly moved her belongings from her previous smaller room into Felicity's suite.

On her lap was the dress, and in her hands—her nail scissors.

It was sacrilege, really, to be hacking away at the lining of a clearly obscenely expensive dress, but she had no other option. Two stylists—for her hair and make-up—were arriving any minute, so she needed to make this dress fit *now*.

It did occur to her that palaces probably had things like royal tailors, or assistants who could dash into the town to buy her more event-appropriate underwear (she wore a well-worn nude strapless bra that was usually beneath nothing more glamorous than a vest top and a pair of cotton knickers printed with purple violets) but she hadn't thought to ask the Prince—no, *Marko*—about them before he'd left the suite looking all relieved and gorgeous.

And so she carefully cut through the figure-hugging dark emerald lining that had been designed to fit a figure with far slimmer hips than hers.

Lining removed, she tried the dress on again.

This time—it made it over her hips. The waist, thank God, fitted perfectly, and the bodice…well… nothing that a few tissues shoved inside her bra wouldn't fix.

Jas straightened her shoulders as she twisted and turned in front of the mirror. It was, honestly, the most beautiful thing she'd ever worn. Its skirt—thankfully made up of enough layers that the lack of lining seemed to make no difference— made lovely swishing sounds as she moved, the silk unbelievably luxurious against her skin. And the gold—and she was pretty sure it was *actually* gold—belt glittered underneath the bathroom lights.

She nodded at herself in the mirror. *Done.* Now, shoes.

She gathered up the heavy fabric of the skirt and headed into the bedroom. On the bureau near the door was a white box labelled with a high-end shoe brand, and inside was a stunning pair of gold heels—that she immediately realised were a size too small.

Why hadn't she checked earlier?

Maybe because she didn't know what the hell she was doing?

Jas met her own gaze in the mirror above the spindly table.

What have I got myself into?

There was a sharp rap on the door, followed by Simon's voice—as he was now, ridiculously, *her* bodyguard. 'Hair and make-up are here,' he said.

'Just a minute!' she said.

Then she scanned the room, wondering if maybe palaces were like hotels—and there would be a phone line directly through to a concierge who could go find her some shoes.

Unsurprisingly, there wasn't.

Again, she met her gaze in the mirror, and again, she straightened her shoulders.

She took a deep breath.

She'd agreed to do this. She'd agreed to do this because she was about to earn her company's entire income from last year in three months—and… because her myriad concerns with saying yes hadn't seemed so compelling when contrasted with the desperation in Prince Marko's gaze.

It hadn't been overt, but she'd seen it. Flashing

in and out so briefly before he'd gathered himself again.

Desperation…and also…*vulnerability*. A vulnerability she'd somehow known he'd hated to reveal. But then—he didn't want to be doing any of this, did he? He didn't want to be desperately asking a total stranger to help him, because he'd much rather his brother was healthy and he didn't have to worry about royal balls and acting kingly. Prince Marko wasn't doing this for himself.

He was asking her to do this crazy, ridiculous thing for his brother, and for Vela Ada.

That was why he'd *needed* her to say yes.

And in the end that was what it had come down to.

Because he'd needed her, she'd said yes. A man she barely knew.

It was nuts. Completely out of character for her to be so impulsive.

And yet she'd done it.

For the next three months, she was Prince Marko of Vela Ada's fiancée.

It might not entirely make sense to her—but she was committed now.

And as such—she was committed to sorting out a pair of sparkly shoes.

She opened the door. Outside stood two very stylish-looking women, and Simon.

'Simon, can you please notify Ivan that I require a pair of gold heels in size nine, with a three-inch heel?'

To Simon's credit, he nodded as if this were a perfectly normal request from his boss.

Then she turned to the stylists. 'Ladies, I'll just change into a robe and be right with you.'

'No problem,' said the older lady, with an American accent, 'Your High—' She paused, then blushed. 'Oh! That probably isn't right yet, is it? What should we call you?'

'Just Jas, is fine,' said Jasmine. 'I'm certainly not royalty.'

'Not yet,' said the woman with a grin.

Your Highness.

Oh, wow. Oh, God.

What had she done?

Marko gripped the carved balustrade tightly, his gaze aimed unseeing at the stairs that would lead him to the ballroom two floors below him. He rocked slightly on his heels on the plush carpet, only peripherally aware of the muffled sounds of the string quartet warming up in the distance.

This was both the best, and worst, idea he'd ever had.

As a method to calm his brother during a very stressful time, inventing a fake fiancée was genius. But in every other way it was far from brilliant.

His plan had felt complicated enough when he'd had a trained actress on board. Now…

Now it felt messy.

Now he'd somehow talked Jasmine Gallagher into something he knew she couldn't possibly comprehend. Yes, she'd alluded to the fact she'd be lying to her family, and yes, she was concerned for her business—but she had no idea what it actually meant to be under public scrutiny every moment of the day.

It was life in a fish bowl: a life that he had determinedly escaped. And now Marko had led another woman straight into it, and a woman who—unlike Felicity—didn't welcome the opportunity for a higher profile.

And so he felt bad about that.

But not bad enough to call it off.

Inside his tuxedo jacket, he had a contract for Jasmine that would minimise some of the messiness of the situation with clear expectations and details of his generous remuneration. It was, after all, just a business arrangement. An unusual one, but nothing more—

'Marko?'

He turned at Jasmine's voice, soft—but clear—across the empty landing.

He opened his mouth to say something—but instantly forgot what.

She looked…stunning.

Suddenly, his previous assessments of Jasmine as pretty, or attractive, seemed embarrassingly inadequate.

As did his inability to even notice her until today. He must have been temporarily blind—or his libido temporarily in hibernation—for Marko to have been so oblivious of Jasmine Gallagher.

He swallowed as she shifted her weight, still a good five metres or so away from him—a wide expanse of carpet between them.

The dress was gorgeous. He'd known that—had been involved tangentially in selecting it if you could count Ivan asking him to approve the designer Felicity had chosen—but on Jasmine it was something else. Her skin—so pale—contrasted against the deep emerald fabric, and her hair—so dark—rolled into a lush smooth arrangement at her nape was a sharp contrast to the severely scraped-back ponytail she'd sported earlier today.

Her eyes—still lovely—seemed even larger, and her lips—in ruby red—were lush and glossy.

He watched as she shuffled on the spot again, and then deliberately straightened her shoulders. 'Please say something,' she said, catching his gaze with a piercing look. 'Do I look okay? I feel like the biggest fraud.'

Marko covered the distance between them in a moment, and now he stood close enough that she needed to tilt her chin upwards.

'*Lijep,*' he said. '*Tako lijepo.*'

Jasmine swallowed. 'Pardon me?' she asked.

'Beautiful,' he said, having not even realised he hadn't been speaking English. 'So beautiful.'

'Oh!' she said, looking mildly stunned. 'Thank you. That's a very nice thing to say.'

'It's true,' he said. 'You look like a princess.'

She grinned. 'I suppose that's the idea,' she said. 'You look very much like a prince, yourself.'

Her gaze flicked over his tuxedo—the crisp white shirt, the black bow tie, the white pocket square.

'No crown?' she asked, her eyes sparkling.

'*No,*' he said, firmly. His brother had worn one at his coronation, but Marko never had. But he then surprised himself by adding, 'Damn uncomfortable things.'

How did this woman do that? He'd spent the whole week knotted up with tension, and yet now he was teasing her?

Jasmine's lips quirked upwards.

'Well, I am *actually* uncomfortable in these shoes.' She gathered up her skirt so she could poke her heels out from under the fabric.

They were a glittering gold, with a peep-toe front.

'I didn't have time to paint my toenails,' she continued. 'But these were the best match for the dress out of the collection that Ivan somehow sourced for me. It's just they pinch a little. I have no idea how he did it so quickly. It was like he had some secret stash of evening shoes in the palace.'

'Thank you,' Marko said, suddenly.

She shrugged. 'It's okay, I've packed a few plasters in my clutch so my feet will survive. I'm always prepared.'

She was deliberately misinterpreting him, and it made him smile.

'You know what I mean,' he said.

She just smiled. She was quick to smile—and it was a gorgeous smile. Natural and wide.

How had he not noticed before?

'We have somewhere to be,' she said.

'Ah,' he said, 'the schedule.'

She nodded. 'We need to get moving, or my guys downstairs will get twitchy.'

Almost on cue, a member of Lukas's staff came up the stairs, his boots a soft thud on the carpet. 'The King is ready to see you now.'

They were to meet King Lukas and Queen Petra in the Knight's Hall.

Located at the base of one of the four circular... towers? Turrets? Jas wasn't sure, but whatever they were they were large, and round, and located at the four corners of the palace, connected together by long, stone corridors, half clad in dark wood panelling.

Lukas's attendant had announced their arrival, and then quietly disappeared. No security stood at the opened door before them—at such a secure location, there was no need for it. It was why Prince Marko and herself had no escort, and why Jas's team were already down in the ballroom.

To be honest, on nights like tonight, in a secure building, with a strict guest list and no current threat, there wasn't a heck of a lot for security to do. The King's own staff had the perimeters under control—so all Jasmine and her team would be doing tonight was ensuring that events progressed as scheduled, and to keep an eye out for anything unusual. Effectively, they would've just blended into the background—ready if required, but otherwise unobtrusive. The Prince and Felicity would've barely noticed they were there.

Jas certainly hadn't expected to be anywhere near this close to Prince Marko this evening.

She looked up at him, standing so close to her that her shoulder would bump his upper arm if she moved even a little bit.

No. She certainly hadn't expected to be this close to Marko. Tonight, or ever.

'You okay?' he asked, his voice low.

This close, his delicious accent gave her shivers, and she closed her eyes as she took a deep breath.

'Of course,' she said.

She wiggled her toes in her new shoes, welcoming the way they rubbed just a little at the back—the slight pain a useful reminder that this was *actually* happening. She opened her eyes—only to find herself gazing directly into Marko's blue gaze.

She shivered again.

The sound of a man clearing his throat made Jas jump, and she stepped back abruptly from Marko.

'You two lovebirds planning on joining us?'

It was, of course, the King.

Marko's older brother stood in the opened doorway. He was tall—about the same height as Marko, and with similar dark-coloured hair. But Lukas's hair was longer, and peppered with grey. He wore an identical suit to his brother, but he wore it with an ease that Jasmine only now realised that Marko lacked. Lukas wore his tux as if he wore one every day—and, Jas realised, that probably wasn't too far off the truth. A king must attend formal events as regularly as Jas had Thai takeaway when she was back home: i.e. a *lot*.

Jasmine straightened her shoulders and smiled at Lukas. He was easy to smile at—his expression open and welcoming, so different from his more shuttered brother.

And then Marko wrapped his fingers around Jas's hand—and she had to do everything in her power not to gasp.

Fortunately, Lukas had already turned away, gesturing for them to follow him into the Knight's Hall.

Marko had never touched her before—if she excluded a brief, firm handshake when they'd first met several days ago. Marko had barely met her eyes back then, and as such the touch had been warm—but utterly unmemorable.

This was *nothing* like that.

Marko had laced his fingers through hers—an

intimate gesture, and fitting, of course, for an engaged couple. But for Jas, the intimacy was shocking, and sent a thrill of sensation up her arm and through her body to finally pool low in her belly.

Jas's gaze flew upwards, but Marko wasn't even looking at her. That probably would've dumped ice water over her unwanted reaction—but then, he squeezed her hand.

Now, she *knew* he was just being reassuring. She *knew* he was holding her hand for show and not any other reason.

And yet…as crazy as this was, as *insane* as it all was, it was so easy, just for a moment, to desperately wish it were all real.

But—since when had Jas Gallagher believed in fairy tales?

Inside the Knight's Hall, Jas gently tugged her hand free. She wiggled her toes again, rocking her heels on the parquet floor.

Queen Petra stood near the unlit fireplace, and she turned to greet them. She wore a stunning red gown, and her blonde hair was piled in an elaborate updo, behind a diamond and platinum tiara.

'Hello,' she said, 'I'm Petra.'

She sounded so normal, as if they'd met at a barbecue, except that she had a fancy accent.

'I'm Jasmine,' Jas said. Something terrifically

obvious suddenly occurred to her. 'I'm sorry, am I supposed to curtsey?'

They all laughed. 'No,' Marko said. 'I should've explained. When no one's watching, there's no need for any pomp and ceremony.'

'Absolutely not,' said Petra. 'We're all really normal, actually.'

'Hmm...' was all Jasmine could manage. She was standing in a turret or a tower, with oversized lancet windows, walls full with oil paintings of previous monarchs, and there was a *full suit of knight's armour* standing beside one of the armchairs. 'Normal' didn't really explain any of this.

Lukas laughed. 'Come on, you've been with Marko for six months, you must know by now there isn't anything special about him.'

Marko grinned. 'No, she's already pointed out that I don't have any of your kingliness.'

'Kingliness?' Lukas laughed out loud. 'I like it. I do try my best to be suitably kingly at all times.'

Jasmine silently waited for the floor to open up and swallow her.

Petra saved her. 'Ignore them,' she said. 'Walk with me to the ballroom and tell me all about yourself—I need to know all about the woman who has captured my brother-in-law's heart.'

Petra headed out of the room, obviously expecting Jas to follow. Jas looked to Marko—but he nodded that she should go.

His smile had fallen away, Jas noticed—as had Lukas's.

For the first time, Jas remembered how sick the King was.

'Jasmine?' Petra prompted, and Jas hurried to catch up.

'Can you tell me when I'm supposed to curtsey and stuff tonight?' she asked as they traversed the hallway, skirts rustling in tandem. 'Marko said it didn't matter, but it does to me.'

A white lie, but this level of detail hadn't occurred to her when she'd agreed to this charade.

'Of course,' Petra said. 'I had to learn all this too. It does get easier, I promise. One day it'll be second nature for you.'

'I can't imagine it,' Jas replied, honestly.

Petra paused when they reached the end of the corridor, standing in the palace's huge entry foyer. Behind her twin staircases swept upwards to meet at the first-floor landing and the biggest chandelier Jas had ever seen glittered above them, making the marble floor shimmer and sparkle. Around them palace staff bustled busily, with guests due to arrive any moment.

'Really,' Petra said. 'One day I woke up and the palace felt like home.'

Home?

Jas smiled, relieved she could finally be completely honest. 'I'm sure this place will never feel like home to me.'

After all, in three months' time she'd be back in her real home, and this palace—and this night—would feel like no more than a dream.

CHAPTER FOUR

IT WAS GOING WELL, Marko thought.

For a prince pretending to be engaged and a bodyguard pretending to be in love with him.

His lips curved upwards as he settled back into his chair and absently swirled his champagne.

Actually—that was unfair. Jasmine was doing remarkably well, considering there had been no time to really tell her anything.

He observed her as she spoke to one of the ministers of the Vela Ada parliament, her head tilted as she listened intently to whatever the other woman was saying. The pair stood only a short distance away, between the as yet empty dance floor and one of the many round tables that seated a mix of the most prominent and influential citizens of Vela Ada—from politicians, to philanthropists to entrepreneurs.

Although he'd stood beside Jasmine as they'd greeted the guests with his brother and Petra, and also sat beside her at dinner—they'd barely spoken.

Petra seemed thrilled to have someone else to discuss the realities of adjusting from civilian to royal life with, and had happily taken Jasmine under her wing. And, of course, pretty much everyone wanted to know about his mysterious fiancée, and so there had been a constant stream of interested guests wishing to introduce themselves. At first, Marko had stood nearby, ready to answer or deflect any tricky questions—but there was no need. Jasmine improvised like the actress she said she wasn't—smoothly redirecting conversation to topics other than the details of their supposed relationship, or answering with laughter and ambiguity, allowing guests to fill in the blanks however they saw fit.

With Jasmine doing so well, it had left Marko free to have his own conversations. Which he had: with a retired army general, a prominent business owner, a former Olympian. They were all nice people, and the conversations were pleasant enough—but it didn't take long for him to be over it. In fact, he'd been over it from the moment he'd stood in that reception line, greeting hundreds of people in a blur of handshakes and a cheek-aching smile.

He'd excused himself and headed for his table—then downed his champagne in one gulp.

A waiter immediately refilled his drink—but he

resisted downing that one too. Someone was always watching at these events, and the last thing he needed was another Playboy Prince non-scandal to disappoint his brother and pretty much everyone else who knew him.

He didn't want to be here.

He *really* didn't want to be here.

What he'd much rather be doing was hanging out with Lukas. To do anything with him—maybe play pool at the table his brother had in his library. Or watch a movie and drink beer. Or just have something nice to eat. Stuff they hadn't done together in longer than he could remember.

And something he wanted to do, with the person he wanted to spend time with—and *not* in public, and not with the weight of expectation and obligation weighing heavily upon him.

But instead he was here, at a ball, to make other people feel better about Lukas's illness, when *he* certainly wasn't feeling any better about it. Talking to Lukas, or to the royal doctor, had done nothing to ease the spiky ball of worry, concern and fear that had lodged itself in Marko's belly.

If he lost him…

Marko clenched his jaw.

No. He wouldn't even consider it. He couldn't.

His gaze travelled back to Jasmine—searching

for a distraction. Maybe she sensed his gaze, as she turned towards him.

She began to smile—but then stopped. Her brow furrowed.

In concern?

He swore under his breath.

He looked away—focusing his attention on his fingers as they gripped the stem of his glass, absently spinning the glass from side to side.

He tensed as Jasmine slid into the chair beside him. He did *not* want to have a conversation about whatever Jasmine had thought she'd seen in his face. Not with a woman he barely knew. Not with anyone.

'Only a few minutes before the speeches,' she said quietly.

He turned in his seat to look at her.

She looked—totally normal. No more furrowed brow. No questions in her gaze.

He felt his shoulders relax. *What was wrong with him?*

He was jumping at shadows.

'You don't need to worry about that,' he said, happy to talk about anything. 'Palace staff will let us know where we need to be.'

'It's still my job,' she said, with a shrug. 'I can't switch it off. I'm keeping an eye on my team, too, although it's weird to not be able to talk to them. I feel naked without my earpiece at a formal event.'

Naked was probably not the best word Jasmine could've chosen. Or possibly it was the *best*, as Marko was now extremely effectively distracted from his unwanted thoughts of Lukas, and royal duty and...

Tako lijepo.

God, she was hot in that dress—all pale skin and soft curves.

He caught Jasmine's gaze again as his crept back up to her face. She narrowed her eyes.

Marko cleared his throat.

This is a business arrangement, he reminded himself.

'Is that why you're so good at talking to everyone?' Marko asked, focusing on not—once again—ogling Jasmine, as she'd so accurately accused him of earlier that day. Could it really have only been today? 'You've attended lots of events like this one?'

Jasmine nodded. 'On the other side, of course,' she said. 'I've been in the background—or at times right on the shoulder—of all sorts of conversations. And I've spoken to all sorts of people too. Some VIPs are chatty in the car, or bored when they're waiting for someone or something, and often I'm the only person available to talk to. I guess maybe I've picked up a few bits and pieces, although this is a bit different from a quick chat to a pop star who's nervous before a performance, or talking to a visiting ambassador about kangaroos.' She reached for her own champagne. 'I'm glad you think I'm doing a good job. I just feel like I'm doing lots of smiling and rambling about not much at all.'

'That's all I do,' Marko said. 'Smile, talk about something benign, then nod at someone else's benign conversation while trying to look interested. Welcome to a royal event.'

She nodded. 'Everyone's been very nice to me. And some of the people I've spoken to are really interesting. But it's not,' Jasmine said in a low voice, leaning closer as if to confide in him, 'quite as exciting as I expected.'

Marko laughed out loud. 'No. Being royal is a job. With really great food and wine, but just a job, nonetheless.'

A palace attendant tapped on Marko's shoulder and murmured in his ear.

He stood, and reached for Jasmine's hand.

'Looks like we're up,' he said.

It was time for Marko to formally introduce Jasmine to Vela Ada.

* * *

Jas hadn't thought to put her champagne glass down before following Marko to the small stage at one end of the ballroom, and so now she stood beside the King and Queen, with Marko, feeling somewhat as if she were about to give a speech at a really, really fancy wedding.

Although—thankfully—she wasn't scheduled to actually say anything. Her role tonight was to stand beside Marko and look like the loving fiancée she supposedly was.

The loving fiancée part wasn't all that hard. It was all too easy to stand, oh, so close to him—close enough to feel his body heat, and to smell whatever delicious fragrance he wore—something crisp and woody.

And to look up at him—to imagine she was in love with him—was easy, too. He still held her hand—and he squeezed it occasionally, sending shivers of sensation rioting throughout her body.

He did so now, and glanced downwards to hold her gaze. His gaze was reassuring, a *you've got this* message. There was nothing more—not a hint of what she'd seen before: both an unexpected rawness of emotion she'd glimpsed as he'd been watching her from a distance, but also a different type of rawness later—that heat, that *wanting*.

She'd tried to shut it down—she'd glared at him, channelling her affront of earlier that day. But as it had been during the briefing, she hadn't really had her heart behind it.

In fact, her heart had been beating at a million miles an hour.

Now she squeezed his hand back. *I'm fine.*

But she wasn't—not really.

Partly, she was uncomfortable simply standing here—while she'd been at many important events in her career, she'd never been the subject of such concentrated attention. Standing beside someone important on a stage, in her black suit, was *not* the same as wearing a ball gown with a room full of dignitaries staring at her.

She felt terribly awkward in her tight shoes and with her superfluous champagne glass, and it was a constant battle not to fidget.

But she didn't, of course. She was a professional. She could do this.

Lukas was speaking now, in the Vela Ada dialect—and as Jas knew only very few words of the Slavic language, she could only guess at what he was saying.

His voice revealed none of his illness, although this close she could see how lean he was beneath his suit, and the hint of dark beneath his eyes.

Petra stood beside him, looking composed and lovely. And she *was* lovely, and had been all evening to Jas—checking in with her, whispering little hints and words of encouragement. Earlier she'd even given her a crash course in curtseying—although with the only other royals in attendance being the late King Josip's brother and his wife, as Lukas and Marko's mother had retired from public life following her husband's death, she'd only had to worry about it briefly—and in the end it hadn't been that hard at all.

But it was Petra that she was feeling most uncomfortable about—more so than feeling awkward in front of hundreds of guests. Here was a woman dealing bravely with her husband's cancer diagnosis, and Jas was—*lying* to her.

Marko leant down to murmur in her ear, his breath a tickle against her skin. 'Here we go.'

Lukas gestured for Marko to step forward, and Jas stepped up right beside him.

'And now,' Lukas said, in English now, 'I'd like to introduce the woman who will be accompanying Prince Marko as he takes on my royal commitments over the next three months—and who I am looking forward to welcoming into the Pavlovic family: his fiancée, Jasmine Gallagher.'

The ballroom filled with polite applause, and Jasmine just smiled and tried not to look awkward.

Marko then began to speak—again, in Slavic, and as he spoke—and he spoke well—Jasmine took the opportunity to simply watch him.

He stood tall, and powerfully—his shoulders back, his stance firm—and there was definitely no fidgeting involved. He looked fantastic in his suit, but it did nothing to hide the strength of the man, the solid contour of his biceps and the width of his shoulders evident beneath the expensive fabric. His buzz-cut hair only further enhanced the impression of a man constructed of hard edges—there was no softness to this prince.

She'd noted before that he wore his suit less comfortably than his brother, and she still thought that true. There was a tension to Marko's posture, as if he was out of his native habitat. He'd said earlier that a royal title was just another job, and although she didn't think it was that simple—there were some big perks to being a royal!—she understood his sentiment. And so—knowing he was a highly ranked military officer—she supposed it was army fatigues rather than a tuxedo that was his uniform of choice?

And yet, despite his incongruity in a tuxedo, and despite the tension she sensed in him—and also whatever it was she'd glimpsed in his gaze earlier—he now commanded the ballroom. His ability to do so wasn't unexpected—since she'd met Marko it had been impossible to ignore his magnetism—but *before* she'd met him, she wouldn't have expected it.

She had thought her company had been hired to protect a playboy prince—and the Playboy Prince she had expected was nothing like Marko at all.

Of course she'd seen the photos of Marko in women's magazines. And of course she'd looked him up on the Internet again when she'd first been approached to work for him. And the photos and articles were all the same: about a man who had eschewed a royal life to flit across Europe—and who had seemingly never been photographed with the same woman twice. There he'd been, on the list of World's Most Eligible Bachelors or the World's Hottest Royals or whatever.

None of this had mattered to her, as it had no impact on the job she'd been hired to do.

But she'd been curious.

Even the whole fake fiancée ruse hadn't really given her pause—she and her team had just signed the water-tight confidentiality agreement and been done with it. It wasn't her job to judge the decisions of the rich and famous—no matter how odd or misguided they appeared to her.

Of course, it *had* given her pause when Marko had asked her to take Felicity's place.

Suddenly Marko's lie would be affecting her. And now Marko's lie was *her* lie. She was no longer a bystander—she was part of this.

Ever since her impulsive decision to be Marko's fake fiancée, the weight of that lie had only grown heavier the more real it had become.

And standing here right now, in front of hundreds of people as a man you barely knew announced you to his *country* as something you weren't…well, lies didn't get much bigger than that.

What have I done?

Were the pleas of a man who made her blood run hot enough of a reason to do something so far outside her moral compass?

His reasons at the time had seemed so compelling, the lie so harmless…

But now…

Jas's gaze flicked from Marko back to Lukas.

As she watched he stepped back from where he'd stood beside Marko.

Marko noticed—although to anyone in the crowd they'd never know.

But Jas saw it. She saw the nearly imperceptible

inclination of Lukas's head towards Marko, and then Marko's matching gesture back.

Lukas took Petra's hand—and Jas saw how tightly he gripped it. Then he closed his eyes, and released what she imagined was a long-held breath.

Relief.

Petra leant in close to kiss her husband's cheek, and when she turned back to look again at Marko her eyes were glazed with unshed tears.

'Jasmine?'

Marko's voice made her jump, and to her horror it also made the long-forgotten champagne glass dislodge from her fingertips.

It shattered loudly at her feet, to a chorus of gasps from the crowd.

And then—before her brain could catch up with all that it had been coping with today: fake princesses, and ball gowns, and curtseys, and unwell kings, and friendly queens and the way Marko's voice and touch just did all sorts of *things* to her—she swore.

Rather loudly.

CHAPTER FIVE

THE ENTIRE BALLROOM went absolutely silent, after a few bursts of laughter were quickly muffled.

Jasmine's expression as her gaze shifted from the shards of glass at her feet to meet with Marko's own was of pure mortification.

Her lovely mouth had dropped open, and her already pale complexion had turned completely white.

'Marko—I am *so* sorry,' she said, barely above a whisper. 'I don't even really swear that often, honestly, and then to say *that*, here... I don't know what came over me. Oh, God, now I've embarrassed you, and your family, let alone myself and—'

Her words were getting all jumbled—so he reached out, grabbed her hand, and tugged her close to his side. Her eyes widened, but she went silent.

He leant close to her, and whispered roughly, 'Can I kiss you?'

'Pardon me?'

'Let's give them something else to remember

about the first time they met Prince Marko's fiancée.'

She just blinked at him.

'Jasmine?'

'You want to kiss me? Right here, in front of hundreds of people?'

He just smiled at her. And *looked* at her—right into those lovely hazel eyes.

He supposed, in theory, it was a *don't-stress-about-it*-type kiss. At least—that was his intention.

He was playing the role of the loving, supportive fiancé, after all.

But also—yes, he wanted to kiss her. If he was honest with himself, he'd wanted to kiss her ever since she'd told him off in that briefing.

She closed her eyes, and he watched as she took a deep breath.

When she opened them, she nodded.

And then—he kissed her.

So it was a simple kiss—a straightforward kiss.

His mouth pressing against hers briefly, nothing more.

But then—when his mouth did touch hers—suddenly, it wasn't brief. Suddenly—he lingered.

Her lips were soft, and fleetingly cool beneath

his own. They were chastely closed, of course—but they shifted against the pressure of his own mouth, as if she'd open her mouth for him if only he were to ask.

It was shockingly, unexpectedly sexy—a simple kiss that felt like a promise of so much more. It wasn't just about the touch of their lips or the mingling of their breathing—but of the subtle movement of their bodies, the way they leant towards each other while still only joined by their laced fingers.

Marko was no longer aware of their audience, or of the ballroom, or even why he'd kissed her in the first place.

All that mattered was the way her mouth fitted so perfectly against his.

Something—maybe a cough, or a sigh, or a laugh—dragged Marko backed to reality, and he ended the kiss. But he didn't move far—instead he leant even closer, and in a low, gravelly, drawn-out whisper only she could hear he repeated the exact same curse Jasmine had so loudly exclaimed just minutes earlier.

She laughed, breathily, as he turned back to the podium, and introduced Jasmine Gallagher to Vela Ada.

* * *

The evening breeze ruffled diaphanous curtains as Jasmine stepped through one of the several open French doors that led onto the palace terrace.

The terrace was wide and paved with large flat stones, criss-crossed with decorative lines and swirls of cobblestones. With the sun now set the terrace was lit only by the ballroom behind her, and the many strings of fairy lights that decorated the castle architecture—wrapping around pillars and arches and outlining the notches in the crenelated wall that edged the terrace—and the palace.

In daylight, Jasmine knew, she'd be able to see across the city of Vela Ada—across its undulating sea of red-roofed cottages and out to the pure white sand beaches and the Adriatic Sea.

But tonight she could barely see the outlines of some of the giant trees that grew beside the palace—instead they were simply black shadows against a sparkling, starry sky.

Jas shivered, even though it was a mild late summer evening.

She was alone. And thanks to a quick word to her team, she would remain so.

She took a long, deep breath in an attempt to slow her turbulent thoughts.

She closed her eyes.

No. That was a mistake.

Closing her eyes only reminded her of how her eyes had slid shut as Marko's lips had covered hers.

Her eyes snapped open.

A kiss. It was just a kiss.

For show only.

And as a show, it had been immediately effective. During the kiss itself—which could have taken place over five seconds or five minutes, Jasmine had no idea—she'd been oblivious to her surroundings. But after Marko had stepped away it had been immediately obvious that the mood of the room had shifted.

From a mood that Jas had interpreted as a mix of censure, laughter and pity, the room had transformed into warm approval—as if Marko had beguiled the room as well as Jasmine.

No.

She wasn't beguiled by Prince Marko.

She was *working* for him.

So what if he'd dealt with her clumsiness in the most perfect way, and then introduced her to his people as if he were truly in love with her—with pride and admiration that would've made Jas melt into a puddle of happiness should any of it actually have been real?

That the Playboy Prince was charming was of no surprise to her.

But that he was considerate, and, despite his reputation, clearly extremely loyal to both his brother and Vela Ada—this was a little unexpected.

And that he was a fabulous kisser…

Wait. No, that wasn't surprising. That he'd kissed *her*. Yes—that was surprising.

That was about the last thing she'd ever imagined would happen to her.

Kissed by a prince.

'Jasmine?'

She turned at Marko's voice. He stood across the terrace—a step or two down from the French doors, only his silhouette visible with the bright lights of the ballroom behind him.

Unfortunately, she hadn't been able to ask her team to keep Marko away. Mainly because it would've looked seriously weird if anyone had noticed, and partly because she did *not* want her team to realise how flustered she was by that kiss.

She was a professional, after all.

Even if she smashed champagne glasses and swore at the most regal and formal of events anyone could ever imagine…

Mentally she gave herself a shake. It was done now. Time to move on.

Even if she could've done with some more Marko-free time. Having him even this close to her had her all prickly and tingly with awareness. It was exceedingly distracting.

'I think it's definitely time you just called me Jas,' she said, and was pleased that she sounded satisfactorily relaxed and normal. Professional.

'Jas,' he said, as if testing it out on his tongue. With Marko's accent, her name sounded about as exotic as it ever, possibly could.

He crossed the terrace, and as he drew near Jas was able to make out his features in the moonlight—the sharp shape of his nose, the strength of his jaw, and the outline of the mouth she'd kissed just minutes ago.

'I'm sorry,' she said abruptly, needing to halt her wayward thoughts. 'About the glass. And the swearing.'

'I know you are,' Marko said. 'But it doesn't matter. That entire room now believes we're in love, and that's all that matters. That is—' he'd stopped now, close enough that if she reached out she could touch the expensive wool of his suit '—if you've decided if you're going to continue in this role or not.'

Jas blinked, surprised. 'You think that's why I came out here?'

She wrapped her arms around herself, rubbing at the wave of goose pimples that dotted her skin.

'Yes,' he said firmly. 'You're having second thoughts.' A statement.

She nodded, because he was right. Or almost right. 'I am,' she said. Then swallowed. 'I mean— I was.'

Something shifted in Marko's posture—a silent exhalation of relief?

'It's all the lying,' Jas said. 'I was worried about lying to my friends and family, but I hadn't thought about how I'd feel about lying to people face to face. Especially people who are close to you, like Lukas and Petra. I feel terrible about it, especially given what they're going through.'

Now Marko nodded, but made no comment.

'But then I saw the way Lukas responded when you took the microphone tonight. It was like the weight of the world had been lifted from his shoulders. And that's when I got why you're doing this— it's all for Lukas. Not Vela Ada, but Lukas.'

'It's the weight of Vela Ada he has on his shoulders,' Marko corrected her. 'He's been carrying it alone for a very long time.'

His gaze flickered away from Jas's as he spoke, and she wondered at his last sentence. But before she could say or ask anything, he continued.

'And yes—you're correct. This is all about Lukas. I couldn't give a damn what anyone else thinks of my reputation, but it does matter to me when Lukas believes it. He sees me as self-indulgent and unreliable. An outsider from the royal family who has shunned all my princely responsibilities.'

'But your stellar military career—'

'Doesn't hide the fact I've avoided anything to do with the palace for as long as I, or anyone else, can remember,' he finished for her. 'I'm not going to sugar coat it, Jas—I've left it all to my big brother to deal with. Lukas knows it—*everyone* knows it. My army career doesn't cancel that out.'

'Okay,' she said. It was about all she could think of to say. She couldn't really comprehend the idea of having to bear such responsibilities purely due to the circumstances of your birth.

'So,' he said, 'thank you—once again—for doing this for me. With you, I appear a changed man. And that's exactly my goal.'

He smiled at her—a gorgeous, grateful and, as always, sexy smile—and not for the first time this evening, Jas was losing herself in his eyes.

Then, Jas watched as Marko quickly undid a single button of his jacket. In the darkness his black waistcoat seemed to blend into his jacket, and his shirt was as white as the moon.

It took her a moment to realise that he was holding his lapel to show her the lining of his jacket. Part of a white envelope poked out of an inside pocket.

'I've had Ivan write up a new contract—based on Felicity's, and it contains the contract terms and your remuneration details.'

A contract. Money. Of course.

What else had she thought Marko was doing?

She mentally gave herself a little shake—*clearly* it had been too long since she'd had a date if a man unbuttoning his suit jacket made butterflies flutter inside her.

'The confidentiality statement is a little more comprehensive than the one you've already signed, and it also outlines your role in more detail than what we've discussed.'

Jas nodded, but she was trying to remember when her last date was. Surely it wasn't that long ago? It had been in London, at the end of a short four-day job with an international cellist. She'd had a really nice dinner—a rack of lamb with this amazing rosemary breadcrumb crust and…what was his name again?

It was probably not great that she'd remembered

her meal but not the name of her date. Although that was probably also unsurprising as she'd just realised that it had been over a year ago. Fourteen months, to be exact.

Marko was still explaining the contract, and she *knew* she should be paying attention. But she'd read it later anyway before she signed it, and right now she needed to reassure herself that it was simply *logical* that one kiss from a prince had her all starry eyed—just through the lack of any form of romantic male contact in so long.

It wasn't anything about Marko, especially.

'It details all the responsibilities of the role, including, of course, the kissing policy, amongst other things—'

It was important to Jas that Marko's kiss *wasn't* special, because she'd already learnt the hard way how badly professional life and relationships could conflict. Plus, while—

Wait. Kissing policy?

'Pardon me?'

Marko's teeth were a perfect white as he smiled. 'Just seeing if you were paying attention.'

'So there isn't a kissing policy?' Something else occurred to her, and she added more stridently, 'Or an *anything else* policy?'

Marko had long ago let his jacket fall closed, and

now he raised his hands in mock surrender. 'I assure you there is not. I would never ask you to do anything that you didn't want to do.'

She thought back to those moments after she'd smashed that glass: *Can I kiss you?*

No, he wouldn't ask her to do anything she didn't want to do.

It was impossible in the fairy-light-lit almost darkness to read Marko's gaze, but in the silence he was definitely looking at her.

She sensed, rather than could clearly see, his lips curve into a grin.

Had he stepped closer?

Suddenly the air between them felt hotter—and infinitely more electric.

'Unless,' Marko began, and his voice was all low and impossibly even sexier than normal, 'you would like there to be a kissing policy?'

The atmosphere fairly crackled now.

Had she moved closer? Someone definitely had, as no longer would she need to reach far to touch the fabric of his suit. Not very far at all.

A sudden breeze made the towering trees beside the terrace rustle in the darkness, but the sound barely registered in Jas's periphery.

Instead, her gaze remained on Marko, and, while she desperately wished she could see him more clearly, there was no questioning the hotness of his gaze, or her certainty that Marko would be seeing a matching heat in hers.

It would be so, so easy to close the gap between them. To run her fingers along the fine wool that covered his broad shoulders and then entwine her hands behind his neck. To allow herself to fall into him—to press her body close against his, and to kiss him very differently from before. This time with open lips and tongue and…

'You mean a no-kissing policy?' Jas said suddenly, and sharply, brutally yanking her traitorous libido back to reality.

And the reality was that this was *not* real. Prince Marko was a client. She was a professional.

Marko stepped back.

'You can have Ivan add it to the contract if you wish,' he said, not missing a beat.

As if the last few minutes had never happened. As if Jas had imagined the almost magnetic pull that she'd felt between them.

Jas straightened her shoulders.

Thank goodness she'd pulled herself together before she'd done something stupid.

He was the Playboy Prince, after all.

He probably seduced every woman he met. She'd just happened to be the closest one available.

And the fact she hadn't felt that way—that he'd made her feel special rather than one of many—was just a mark of what a player he was.

'We'd better get back inside,' Marko said. 'We don't want to miss out on dessert. Have you had Vela Adian pastries before? Our chef is famous for his *pršurate* and *hroštule*.'

Jas just nodded and followed Marko back inside. At the top of the steps, and just before they walked through those gauzy curtains again, he took her hand in his. Once again he casually laced his fingers with hers, and once again he smiled at her.

Still that made her heart do a little flip.

But she ignored that entirely, and instead smiled right on back.

And silently decided that she *would* be adding that no kissing clause.

It would make things between them crystal clear.

There would be no more kisses from the Playboy Prince.

CHAPTER SIX

MARKO FOUND JAS sitting at the only table on the dining room terrace the next morning.

Her attention was focused on her open laptop, and she didn't immediately notice his approach.

She sat at the table where the King and Queen generally had breakfast together, but Lukas and Petra had left early that morning for the Pavlovic Estate where they'd be based during Lukas's treatment. It was also the table where the previous King and Queen—Marko's parents—had taken their breakfast.

'My mother and father used to like sitting here,' Marko said when he stood beside Jas. 'My mother used to get Lukas and me to count all the boats we could see in the harbour.'

Her head jerked upwards at his voice, and she blinked in surprise as she met his gaze. 'Sorry,' she said, 'I was in my own little world.' Then she turned to look out to the ocean. As always, boats dotted the view, and even from this distance Marko could make out colourful towels decorating the white sand of a beach, and a flock of seagulls hovering above the water.

'I can't imagine waking up to this every morning,' Jas said, turning back to Marko. 'My mum's flat had a balcony with a view of the neighbouring building, and I used to eat breakfast cereal in front of the TV while she got ready for work.'

'We had a chef,' Marko said. 'Lukas and I used to ask him to make us dinosaur-shaped pancakes.'

Jas laughed out loud. 'I'm glad I didn't know there were some kids on the other side of the world with their own chef each morning, as otherwise I might not have been so happy with my Weet-bix.'

'But you were?' Marko asked, curious.

'Happy, you mean? With my Weet-bix and a balcony with a herb garden instead of a view?'

He nodded.

'Yes,' she said, now looking at *him*, curiously. 'Very much. It was just Mum and me, but we laughed a lot. Even at the brick view when we first moved in.'

But Marko didn't elaborate, and instead placed his coffee on the table. Jas's brow wrinkled.

'You want to sit with me?' she asked.

'Unless that's a problem?' Marko said, surprised. The kiss last night could've complicated things, but Jas had made her feelings clear with her 'no-kissing' clause.

He had wondered, for more than a moment, if maybe they could build on that kiss they'd shared, and discover where the electricity he'd felt would lead them. Out on that ballroom terrace, it had momentarily been all he could think about.

Sex definitely hadn't been a requirement of his fake fiancée, but it could certainly make things over the next few months more fun.

Or—as he'd belatedly realised—more complicated.

He'd never had a relationship stretch from weeks into months, and so there was no doubt that any physical relationship between himself and Jasmine would come to an end well before Lukas returned. And where would that leave them? Best case, it would end amicably and their business relationship would continue as before.

Worst case, it would end acrimoniously and continuing to persuade Vela Ada they were in love would be impossible.

So, yes—Jasmine's 'no-kissing' clause was definitely a good thing.

Even if he had to remind himself of that as he admired her long legs revealed by denim shorts and tan sandals that criss-crossed just past her ankles.

'Oh, no,' Jas said, shaking her head. 'Of course not. I just didn't expect you to.'

'I think the staff would think it strange if we didn't keep each other company.'

'Oh!' Jas said. 'That makes sense.'

She seemed to relax at that explanation, and she snapped her laptop closed and moved it aside.

'Well,' she said, 'if we have to sit together, it probably is a good idea if we talk a bit about ourselves. You know, the kind of stuff that we should know given we're engaged.'

Marko didn't feel he *had* to sit with Jasmine at all. In fact, he'd come out here because he'd been looking for her—not because of the role she was playing for him, but because he was wondering how she was after last night. After their…uh… *conversation* on the ballroom terrace there'd been little opportunity to talk, and she'd said very little when he'd handed her the contract outside her room later on.

'How are you feeling?' he asked. 'After your first royal engagement?'

Jas tilted her head, as if confused. 'I'm fine,' she said. 'Why wouldn't I be?' She reached for her own coffee. 'Now, let's start with the big questions: how do you like your coffee?'

* * *

Jas had been *almost* glad at Marko's interruption.

Almost, because she'd already determined that time spent with Marko was not exactly relaxing. Around him, she wasn't herself. She wasn't calm, she wasn't together.

She did *not* like that.

But—Marko's interruption had allowed her to save her reply to her mother's email as a draft, rather than finish it. A reply to an email that had consisted of an official palace photo of Jas beside Marko, Lukas and Petra as they'd welcomed guests to the ball, and a subject line of question marks.

That was definitely going to be the worst part of all of this: lying to her mother. She had several missed calls on her phone as well from family and friends—but she'd responded to only one: her mum. Although she'd cheated and called her when she'd known she'd be at her yoga class, and had left a voicemail.

'I'll send you an email and explain everything.'

Explain things how, exactly, Jas?

The confidentiality agreement she'd signed as part of Gallagher Personal Protection Services already meant that telling her the truth was not an option. Her latest contract—which she'd sign once Ivan had added the no-kissing clause she'd requested—only made the requirement for secrecy even more iron clad.

So yes—she'd have to lie to her mum. And so yes—briefly—she'd been glad for Marko's interruption. Even as she'd noticed how fantastic he looked in faded jeans and a T-shirt that did more than hint at the power of his chest and shoulders.

But then when he'd sat down, her tummy had done all that ridiculous flip-flopping again, and it had been concentrating on their *business* relationship—which was, of course, all this was—that had helped her to refocus.

From the coffee discussion, their conversation had flowed to other easy topics: favourite movies, food, holiday destinations. She'd asked him more about his childhood, curious at the almost wistful look in his gaze when she'd mentioned her Weetbix and TV breakfasts. She wasn't even sure if it was possible for Prince Marko *to* look wistful, but the discovery that he'd had private tutors until university helped to make a bit more sense of why the simplicity of her youth might have seemed appealing to him. Although she definitely wouldn't havc said no to 'all you can cat' dinosaur pancakes.

'So why join the police?' he asked.

A member of the palace staff had magically appeared once they'd each finished their coffees, and now fresh coffee and pastries sat between them, their delicious aroma mingling with the clean scent of the giant firs that surrounded the palace.

Jas smiled. She'd been asked this a million times before.

'I always knew I would,' Jas replied. 'Since I was a little girl. My mum and I didn't have a lot of money, and for a long time after my dad left we were waiting for public housing. So we both slept on couches, always feeling like an imposition on mum's friends and acquaintances and hyper-aware of overstaying our welcome. We had absolutely no control over our situation, and I hated it, and I hated how much my mum worried.'

She reached for one of the pastries—a piece of strudel packed with apples, sultanas and cinnamon.

'So, I guess it's no surprise that I grew up into someone who likes to be in control of things. And for some reason I thought that if I was in the police, I'd be in control. I mean—of course I was also attracted to the idea of protecting people—and I have a really strong sense of right and wrong, too—but there was a lot about the allure of having authority. Of being in charge in a situation.'

'And is that what you experienced?'

Her lips curved upwards. 'Not the way I expected. There was a lot of frustration too—of being part of some great police work that sometimes led to soft or no sentences for the bad guys. And then there were the people—mostly men—who had real issues with a woman in the force. It was exhausting having to prove myself all the time—to the members of the public who'd talk to my junior male partner more than me, and even within the job itself. When I made it to the ANP, and protecting the Prime Minister, it felt even more like a boys-only club.'

Jas stopped talking, unsure why she was going into so much detail. The Prince didn't need to know all of this.

'So that's why you started your own company?' Marko asked.

No.

Her stomach roiled in a familiar, unwanted, visceral reaction to the real reason she'd left the ANP.

She'd started her own company because she'd made the mistake of falling in love with a sergeant within her department. A man who she'd found out, too late, had definitely not loved her back. A man who'd betrayed her in the most—

'Yes,' she said, forcibly halting the direction of her thoughts. 'That's exactly why I did.'

She'd answered his question completely normally—she seemed to be getting better at channelling her usual, measured self around him—and yet Marko was studying her as if she'd said something he didn't believe.

Jas looked down at the untouched pastry still in her hand. She took a bite, but barely tasted it.

This was the second time in two days that she'd allowed memories of the past to clutter her brain.

But she could *not* allow that.

And so she dusted off the icing sugar that had fallen onto her fingers, and met his gaze again. Steady and assured.

'So,' she asked calmly, 'why did you join the military?'

Now he looked away—out over the trees that covered the hill the palace was built upon. But he was looking at Jas again when he said: 'Because I hated this place.'

Jas felt her mouth drop open, but before she could say anything footsteps alerted her to Ivan's arrival.

'We have an hour before we need to depart for your school engagement, Your Highness, Ms Gallagher.'

Marko nodded sharply, then stood, and left without a word.

* * *

Because I hated this place.

Why would he say that?

He sat in the back seat of one of the fleet of low, dark palace sedans, with Jasmine beside him. They were heading to an elementary school in one of the lower socio-economic townships of Vela Ada, where he'd be representing Lukas at the announcement of a palace-funded literacy programme.

Why would he say that?

His dislike of royal responsibilities was well known, but he'd certainly never said anything like that before. He didn't even think he'd said it to himself privately.

Had he hated growing up in the palace?

Did he still hate the palace now?

He kept asking himself those questions as the car slid over undulating roads that narrowed as they approached the town, but he found himself unable to answer.

By the time the convoy of three cars pulled onto a grassy verge to allow a small truck laden with a family of goats to pass, he'd managed to shove the questions aside.

It didn't actually matter, after all.

Whether he liked the palace or not—and all it

represented—he was living there for the next few months.

That was all that mattered.

The woman he'd be living with for that time was currently chatting to the driver and to the body-guard sitting in the passenger seat.

No—not chatting. She was running through the plan for this school visit, reminding her team of the school's layout from a reconnaissance visit she'd led two days earlier. She then noted the possible exit points should there be any need to evacuate the Prince.

'And his fiancée,' Marko reminded Jas.

She slid a glance in his direction, and her lips quirked upwards. 'I'll be fine,' she said drily.

His gaze flicked over her. She wore a navy blue and white summer dress that was part of a ward-robe of clothing that Ivan had sourced under the guise of lost luggage. Sleeveless, but with a high neck and shirt-style collar, it was fitted to her waist before flaring out to a full skirt that finished not that far above her contrasting pale pink sandals. She looked lovely, with her hair styled into a low bun and swept from her face. But when he met her gaze again, she also looked imminently capable. A woman most definitely still able to do her job, regardless of the height of her heels.

It occurred to Marko, as the car came to a stop outside the school's three-storey building, that in the unlikely event that he and Jasmine *were* attacked by an unknown threat—then with his military training and Jasmine's skill set, there probably didn't exist a more difficult royal target in the world.

He was smiling as the driver opened Jasmine's door, and still was when he joined her on the footpath. He took her hand and laced his fingers with hers in an action that had quickly become second nature to him.

'What are you grinning about?' she asked, tilting her head up to look at him.

It was a warm day, and the sun was hot against his unbuttoned charcoal suit jacket. The sun also made Jasmine's skin glow, highlighting the subtle curves of her biceps and the quiet strength in her lean physique.

'I was just thinking how I almost *want* someone to try and take us down,' he said. 'Good luck to them—you and I would end it before it even started.'

Jasmine gave a shocked, loud laugh, and then clapped her hand over her mouth. When she removed it, she was still grinning. She shoved him in the shoulder with her spare hand.

'You nong,' she said, her eyes twinkling.

'Nong?' he asked, confused.

'You know, like a ning-nong? A bit of an idiot?' She brought her hand to her mouth again. 'Whoops, I'm probably not supposed to call you an idiot, am I?'

But Jas didn't sound at all concerned that she had.

Marko just found himself still smiling at her.

She squeezed his hand, and then, on tiptoes, whispered in his ear, 'While I tend to agree that we *are* pretty well qualified to defend ourselves, I just want to make it clear that you arc *not* to go all superman on me should anything go down. My team is in charge, and you follow our orders, understand?'

He squeezed her hand back. 'Understood.'

She stepped back, just as Ivan loudly cleared his throat.

For the first time, Marko realised there was a small welcoming party—who he knew must be the school principal and local government officials—and about twice as many photographers only a few metres away.

He'd been so focused on Jas, he hadn't even noticed them.

He glanced down at Jasmine, who was still smiling. 'They probably think we were being all lovey-dovey,' she whispered.

He smiled back at her, but he knew he'd never been lovey-dovey in his life.

The school visit was going well, Jas thought.

As far as she could tell, given she could barely understand a word anyone was saying. The kids had seemed really excited to meet Prince Marko, anyway, and Marko himself had seemed pretty relaxed. Certainly more so than at the ball—last night she'd noted the tension in his shoulders and jaw, and today it was barely noticeable. In fact, aside from when one of the journalists had asked a question about the King, rather than the literacy programme, he'd seemed positively content—even laughing along with the kids as he read to a half-circle of nine-year-olds a book illustrated with zoo animals.

Jas didn't feel quite so relaxed. She had no official role—neither had Felicity at any of these events—and so subsequently she simply got to hover near Marko and look…she didn't know. Supportive? Fiancée-like? In love?

Surely Felicity would've been finc, looking effortlessly natural in any surroundings.

Instead, Jas had found herself standing as if she

were on a job—legs just slightly apart, her hands loosely linked in front of her. Her gaze scanned the crowd in the classroom—from Marko and the children and their teachers through to the small bank of invited journalists and photographers huddled at one end of the room.

As always, she was looking at faces and hands, faces and hands, searching for something impossible to define, the slightest sign of something *not quite right...*

Wait. Stop.

She unlinked her hands and gave them a little shake. She shifted her weight and moved her feet closer together.

Her team had the room under control. Today, that wasn't her job.

Her job was to stand still and look elegant. Or something like that.

CHAPTER SEVEN

JAS WAS STANDING beside Marko in the school's entry foyer, preparing to leave, when Ivan approached and murmured something to Marko in Slavic.

Instantly, Jas felt Marko tense.

'No. Not today,' he said. Firmly.

Ivan replied in an urgent whisper, but all Jas could make out was *paparazzi*.

But Marko didn't even reply. Everything in his expression still said *no*.

Ivan might have sighed, but he was too professional to reveal too much in *his* expression. But Jas would guess he was annoyed. Very annoyed.

A moment later Ivan had had a word with Heather from Jas's team—who was leading the team today—but Jas knew what was going on. They were going to be using their alternative exit.

She nodded as Heather explained that paparazzi now congregated outside the school, and how they would reach their new pick-up point, although of course Jas was familiar with it. No matter how low the risk, you *always* had more than one way in and out.

Of course, none of this was unusual. Principals went off-script all the time, and dealing with it was part of her job. And yet…

Why hadn't Marko said something to her?

With Ivan sent out the front to answer a few questions—and act as a distraction—Jas and Marko were led by their protection team out of the school building, once Simon had reported back that the way was clear.

Marko didn't make eye contact with her as they walked.

Which didn't matter, of course. Why should he? He didn't owe her an explanation.

She shouldn't expect one.

But before, outside the school, she'd felt a camaraderie between them. A closeness…

Wait. *Stop.*

If anything she should be annoyed as the head of his protection detail. *Not* as his fake fiancée.

Although she shouldn't be annoyed, because it was her job not to be.

Jas gritted her teeth. She was being *ridiculous.*

Outside, the school was nothing like a typical school back home in Australia. Rather than being surrounded by acres of lush green playing fields, this school was right in the middle of the town, with houses either side in the familiar cream brick, red-roofed style seen throughout the island. Out the back, there was a bitumen-paved play area, painted with lines in overlapping colours to allow for a variety of sports and lunchtime games. Trees lined the tall brick boundary, providing privacy as they walked briskly and silently—but for the tense click of Jasmine's heels.

Through a rear access gate, and down a narrow, cobblestoned laneway—they avoided the most direct route to the street parallel to the school entrance. Instead they continued onwards, behind several terraced cottages, before emerging onto a quiet street perpendicular to the main road—and a moment later their car with its blackest black tinted windows rolled to a stop before them.

They were inside the car, and on their way before it would've even occurred to a single paparazzo that Marko and his new fiancée were taking rather a long time to exit the school.

This was partly because the milling paparazzi didn't expect Prince Marko and his new fiancée to avoid them.

After all, although this particular event had not been publicly announced ahead of time, and school staff and students had been sworn to secrecy, the moment royalty turned up anywhere word was going to get out. And the palace had expected there would be substantial interest in Marko's princess-to-be.

So, while the media inside the school had been palace-selected, and all photographs and content related to the literacy programme would be palace-approved—a relief to Jasmine, given her bodyguard-like behaviour at times—today's schedule had allowed for brief questions from any waiting paparazzi. It was, after all, in Marko's best interests to endear himself to the media given his role was to reassure the people of Vela Ada that all was well, despite Lukas's illness. He needed to be portrayed as competent, approachable...*kingly*, really.

Marko had certainly known this.

And yet here they were—already out of the town and amongst paddocks full of vineyards or dotted with goats.

No one had said a word since they'd left the school building.

Jas desperately wanted to say something now.

But to say what, exactly?

That he should've told her his plans to...well, escape really.

Ideally, yes. He should've. But that was something to debrief him about in private later, not to snap at him now as their car raced through the countryside.

Especially as—and only now, as she observed Marko, did she acknowledge it—Marko still radiated tension.

Mentally, Jas took a step back. This wasn't about her—certainly not about her affront due to not having been informed of what she suspected had been Marko's split-second decision to leave.

It was strange, this sudden escape. As was Marko's reaction to Ivan earlier.

That tension she'd first felt when she'd been standing beside him in the school foyer had definitely not dissipated. Here in the confines of the car, it felt amplified.

None of Marko's body language invited conversation.

But even so, words danced on the tip of Jas's tongue. Different words now—not to lambaste him, but instead to ask him what was wrong.

She felt they'd made progress today: they'd very clearly outlined the ground rules of their business relationship following that somewhat of a *hiccup* at the ball. And they'd had a good chat this morning at breakfast, and Marko had even teased her when they'd arrived at the school.

Teased?

Or flirted with her?

Jasmine dug her fingernails into the palms of her hands.

Nope. She was not going to even *consider* that possibility.

As she needed to keep reminding herself: charming women was what Marko did. It was who he was. He probably flirted so often—anywhere and with anyone—that it was a subconscious reflex.

As she'd determined last night—it was *not* about her.

But even so, they were building a rapport, weren't they? And that was critically important to the success of this ruse.

Although did that mean Marko would welcome her concern?

She doubted it, but still, her eyes traced the hard, angry shape of his jaw uneasily: Marko was *not* okay.

The car jerked slightly as it went over a pothole, and yet Marko remained resolute in maintaining his attention on the lovely—if a little repetitive—surrounding fields.

He couldn't really be any clearer in his wish for silence, but Jas couldn't help herself.

'Marko?' she began.

He spoke—but it wasn't a reply.

'Turn here,' he said, to their driver. It was more of a bark, really. Definitely a demand.

The driver didn't hesitate—lurching the car to a speed capable of making the turn with copious application of the brake, and then accelerating down the un-signposted lane.

'Where are we going?' Jasmine and Heather asked at exactly the same time.

Marko's attention was back out the window. 'This is palace property,' he said curtly. 'We won't be disturbed.'

Heather didn't look very comfortable. Jasmine wasn't comfortable either—she did *not* like going off schedule.

But equally—if they didn't know where they were going, then any threat didn't know either. Their job was to safely get the principal through his day. Wherever that day might take him.

And today, it would seem, it was down a compacted gravel lane, where occasional loose pieces of stone pinged against the underside of this extremely expensive car.

Marko had hoped that when the familiar gravel lane eventually led them to an equally familiar sandy track, he would relax.

But when the car came to a stop—ill equipped for the deep beach sand ahead—he didn't feel even the slightest loosening of the tension that enveloped his neck and shoulders, and caused his head to pound.

Everyone was talking to him—Heather, the driver. They wanted to know what they were doing here, but honestly—wasn't this the point of being a prince? To occasionally do random stuff without explanation?

Actually—not everyone was talking. Jasmine had remained silent since her soft question ten minutes earlier.

He couldn't even look at her.

He'd been aware of her attention since he'd decided to leave the school. At first, he'd sensed her censure—which hadn't surprised him. But later, that censure had shifted to concern. She'd been *worried* about him.

He did *not* like that.

Marko yanked off his dress shoes and socks, rolled up his suit pants, and climbed out of the car and into the salt-tinged air.

It was a decent hike from here to the beach—up and down over several hills that eventually became sparse, scrubby and rocky as the ocean neared.

He shrugged off his jacket, and he gripped it

with white knuckles as he took big strides over that last hill—and could finally see the water.

The sky was cloudless today, perfect above the crystal-clear water of the small, absolutely private beach. Near the shore, he could see straight through to the rocks lining the ground beneath the waves, although about ten metres in the water went sharply from light aqua to deep navy blue, where—as Marko well knew—the water abruptly deepened as suddenly as an underwater cliff.

He and Lukas had swum and snorkelled at this beach their whole lives. Not recently though—it had been…ten years? Or more? He'd been at university, and his father had still been alive.

This place—and the small, hidden cottage that sat set back from the stone outcrops now above him as he negotiated the rocky path down to the shore—had once been the only place Marko had ever felt he could escape to. Lukas had felt the same way.

Here they'd been safe from prying eyes, and from anyone's expectations.

So it should be no surprise it was where he'd gravitated to today.

Now at ground level, Marko clambered over rocks in so many shades of grey—most no bigger in circumference than a dinner plate—a mix of smooth and square and sharp edges.

He remembered the easiest path through the rocks, although he was sure it had been many years since anyone had trod it. He couldn't imagine Lukas here now—his brother was just too important, too busy, too serious.

Finally reaching the coarse sand of the one patch of rock-free beach, Marko sank to the ground, discarding his jacket in a careless pile of charcoal fabric.

And then he put his head in his hands.

He was being an idiot. Such an idiot.

Such an idiot.

What had Jas called him? A nong? A ning-nong?

Well—a far stronger word was required when he'd literally just *run* from the first intrusion of paparazzi he'd had to deal with since his return to Vela Ada. An intrusion he'd expected and yet had, apparently, been unprepared for.

He swore loudly—violently and creatively—at himself and into the sanctuary of this beach that absolutely nobody knew about.

Something—a rock knocking against its neighbour—tugged his attention from his self-flagellation.

It was Jas.

About two-thirds of the way down the steep path to the beach—but facing away from him, as if beating a fast retreat.

He did *not* want anyone on this beach with him.

Jas looked over her shoulder, fleetingly meeting his gaze.

'I'm sorry,' she called out. 'I thought—' A pause, but she didn't elaborate. 'I was wrong. I'm sorry. I shouldn't have disturbed you.'

Then she continued her climb, her long dress flapping in the ocean breeze.

For about another metre.

And then, as Marko watched, a rock beneath Jas's bare feet wobbled dramatically, and despite her arm-waving attempts to regain her balance she crashed to the hard ground with a shocked cry.

In moments, he was beside her, crouching to assess how badly damaged she was.

The breeze had tugged long strands of her dark hair free, and whipped them about her face as she looked up at him.

'I'm fine,' she said, very firmly.

But then she shifted, as if about to get up—and winced.

'You're hurt,' Marko protested.

She shook her head. 'Just give me a moment,' she said. 'It's nothing.'

He watched as Jas wiggled her left ankle—and winced again.

'It's something,' he said grimly. 'Here.'

He stood and offered a hand to assist her up, which she took a moment to grasp.

'I'm really sorry,' she said as she came to her feet, balancing on her uninjured foot. 'You—'

But then she wobbled again, and was suddenly falling towards him.

He grabbed her reflexively, and he wasn't particularly gentle, his hands gripping her firmly at the waist. Even so, he didn't stop her fall entirely, and with a surprised, feminine *oomph* she landed against his chest, her hands sandwiched between them.

There was a long moment of silence.

A long moment where Marko was absolutely aware of everywhere Jas's body was pressed, firmly, against his. They'd kissed last night—but they'd never been this close before. Chest to chest, hip to hip.

Jas flattened her fingers against Marko's chest, but otherwise she didn't move a muscle, her gaze apparently trained on the buttons of his shirt.

'I am *so* sorry,' she said, yet again, but Marko wasn't really paying attention.

Instead, he shifted his hands from her waist, bent his knees—and swung Jas up into his arms.

She gasped against his shoulder as he headed to that small patch of sandy beach—safe from Jasmine's apparent aptitude for identifying hazardous rocks.

There, he sat her down on the sun-warmed sand, and—without giving his actions too much further consideration—sat himself down beside her. He propped his hands behind him, and stretched his legs out alongside Jasmine's.

Then, he looked at her.

Her usually pale skin was tomato red. 'You're blushing,' he said, surprised.

She touched her cheek. 'You think there's a reason I shouldn't be embarrassed after interrupting a clearly private moment, falling on my backside, and then causing a prince a permanent back injury having to heft me down that hill?'

Marko was mildly affronted. 'I can assure you I had no problem carrying you, Jasmine.'

It had been the opposite of a burden having her soft, strong, warm body curled against his chest.

She seemed about to argue with him—but then turned her attention to the horizon. Not a single sail boat interrupted the view.

'This place is amazing,' she said.

He nodded. 'It's a special place for me.'

Her clothing rustled as she attempted to stand again, and he reached out to lay a hand on her leg—on her thigh—to stop her.

Immediately he removed it, not intending his touch to have been so intimate. But, he didn't want her to go.

Or rather, she couldn't go. She'd hurt her ankle. That was it, right?

He rubbed his forehead in exasperation.

'Stay,' he said. 'I don't mind that you're here.'

As he said it, he realised it was true. Only minutes ago he'd grimaced at her unwanted arrival—and yet now her presence was almost comfortable.

But not quite. Because that underlying current between them—and it was constant, no matter what clause they agreed to—hadn't gone anywhere.

That sat together in silence for a while.

It was mid-afternoon, and the sun quickly heated Marko's skin. He removed his tie and made quick work of his shirt—unbuttoning the cuffs and rolling them up to his elbows. His shirt had been pulled out of his dress pants, most likely when he'd picked up Jas, but his skin still prickled beneath his clothing—and if Jas weren't here he probably would've stripped off and dived into the water, and worried about the lack of a towel and other practicalities later.

'I used to come swimming here with Lukas,' he found himself saying, his gaze focused on the crests of the small, lapping waves. 'It felt like the only place on the island where we could totally relax—and where no one was watching.'

'Or asking questions,' Jas prompted. 'Like the media outside the school today.'

Marko shifted to face Jasmine, unsurprised she'd guessed why he'd come here.

'Yes,' he said. 'No paparazzi to bother us here.'

But also no palace staff, and once Lukas was sixteen—no minders. Not one person to observe or comment on their behaviour. Or to advise and pre-empt how they *should* behave.

'Were there more paparazzi than you'd expected today?' Jas asked, her voice gentle.

He didn't want her concern.

'*No,*' he said. 'It was exactly as we'd all expected.'

Her unspoken question seemed to whirl in the breeze: *And so why did you run away, then?*

But he didn't have to answer that. He didn't need to explain anything to Jasmine, or to anyone.

Except…

That he did.

His whole life he'd rebelled against all that was

expected of him. Since adulthood he'd divested himself of pretty much all royal responsibilities, aside from those related to his military career.

But those days were over.

At least, for now.

'Do you know what the paparazzi would've asked us if we'd walked out?' Marko asked, still staring at the waves.

Jas seemed to realise it was a rhetorical question.

'They wouldn't have asked about the literacy programme, or about the kids we met today,' he continued. 'They wouldn't have cared about how investing in literacy will change these kids'—and many other kids'—lives. They wouldn't have cared about anything important.' He paused. 'Instead, they would've asked about your dress. Or your shoes. And I can *guarantee* there would've been some stupid *Playboy Prince* comment—because, of course, that's who they want people to think I am, because it gets them clicks and sells their magazines.'

'And you didn't want to answer those questions?'

'Not today,' Marko said. He rubbed his forehead again. 'Even though I know I need the media on-side. Even though I know I could've just ignored the stupid questions and said my piece about the literacy programme and be done with it. All I needed to do was play nice, and play the role that Lukas needs me to play. Play the game like a good boy. For *once*.'

'But you couldn't,' Jas said neutrally.

Marko waited for the question—for the *Why?*—but it didn't come.

Maybe that was why he decided to explain.

'The first girl I kissed, I kissed at my fifteenth birthday party. It was at the family estate, and not at the palace. We were under this tree practically in the middle of the property, with the lake behind us.'

Jas gasped. 'I know that photo,' she said. 'She had blonde hair, right?' Marko nodded. 'And that was your *first kiss*?'

'Yes,' he said. 'We were over a kilometre from the road, but a photographer with a telephoto lens decided to trespass and he obviously got close enough for that shot.'

'Wow,' Jas said. 'I don't know how I'd feel if my first kiss was documented and then printed and re-printed for the rest of my life. Although, I wouldn't have expected a photographer to be lying in wait behind my local fish and chip shop when Josh from Calculus stuck his tongue down my throat.'

Marko couldn't help but laugh.

'That *is* pretty terrible, though,' Jas said, more seriously now. 'You were still a kid.'

'I was,' Marko said. 'And so was she. It was my first experience being personally targeted by the media. Until then, I'd just been photographed with my parents. This was different. And Sofia—the girl I kissed—was mortified. For a few weeks, she and her family were hounded by the media. It was ridiculous. A private moment—a private memory—was ruined.' He managed a grin now. 'Although I did learn to be more creative with where I kissed girls from then on.'

'I bet,' Jas said drily.

'It didn't stop after that. For some reason, suddenly Lukas and I were being followed everywhere we went. I used to hate how confined I felt in the palace, but now I felt that way *everywhere*. Didn't matter what I did, the media was there. I got drunk for the first time at uni—and there they were. I woke up with a hangover and a headline on the front page of the paper.'

Marko shifted his weight on the sand so he was facing Jas.

She'd pulled her legs up and wrapped her arms loosely around her knees.

'Lukas handled it really well. He just accepted it as part of the deal. I guess he had to—he was the heir to the throne, and so he'd carried that responsibility from birth. He just conformed to what was expected of him. I did try for a while, for a few years at least. But then my father got sick...'

Marko stopped. Swallowed.

'Anyway,' he said, 'eventually I figured, if they want photos of me drinking, or kissing girls—then I'll give them to them.' His lips quirked. 'And also, I was eighteen, so it wasn't like that was a hardship.'

But Jas wasn't smiling with him.

'Your dad had cancer, didn't he?' Jas asked.

'A different type from Lukas,' Marko said firmly. 'And with my father, they think maybe his military service in Vietnam caused—' He stopped again. Swallowed again. 'Anyway. It's different, and treatments are further advanced now, and Lukas's prognosis is excellent.'

He sounded as rehearsed as Lukas's oncologist.

Jas just nodded, and tightened her arms around her knees. He sensed she was trying to work out the right words to say, but that was the thing—there weren't any.

She could hardly reassure him that she was sure Lukas would be okay.

'Look,' Marko said, before she had a chance to say anything. 'The short explanation is: I only found out my brother had cancer this week. I'm doing fine most of the time, but when Ivan told me it was time to go and face those damn stupid questions today, I just couldn't. I couldn't go outside and pander to the media that didn't give a crap about me when they photographed me self-destructing as my father was slowly dying. I couldn't. I—'

His voice cracked. Just like the scared twenty-year-old almost-man he'd once been.

He stood up, and was walking towards the water before he'd even realised what he was doing, his hands unbuttoning his shirt, then his trousers.

In boxer briefs only, he stood for a moment on the smooth rocks in the shallows, the water lapping against his knees.

And then a moment before diving into the water, he looked over his shoulder. At Jas—still sitting on the sand—just looking at him.

'You coming in?' he asked.

CHAPTER EIGHT

JAS HAD NOT joined Marko for a swim.

Common sense had prevailed, as had the reality that she had known this man for less than a week, and that she worked for him. Swimming with Prince Marko in her underwear was *not* an option.

But…oh, it had been tempting.

She'd seen photos of him shirtless before—and after what he'd revealed she felt terribly guilty for being part of the audience that drove photographers to intrude on Marko's life—but those photos really did not reveal how…*devastating* a shirtless Marko was in real life.

She'd known he was fit and strong, and she'd known he had muscles. But she hadn't known the way the sun would paint every hard edge of his body with gold, and she hadn't known how she would feel when the owner of all those delicious hard edges was looking at *her*.

When he'd surfaced after diving into the water…

and that water had sluiced over his broad shoulders and down his pectorals and the occasional dark hair on his chest…

She had literally fanned herself with her hand.

And then quickly stood up, and made her way back to the car. The pain in her ankle now no more than the slightest echo of an ache.

As she'd put the distance between herself and a nearly naked Marko, she'd been able to focus instead on their conversation, and what he'd revealed to her.

Her heart ached as she imagined a teenage Marko grappling with growing up—and later grieving the death of his father—in front of a paparazzo lens. And it ached some more at the emotions the Prince was attempting to deal with now: fear for his brother balanced with the responsibility of acting as Vela Ada's head of state—while faking an engagement.

This was big stuff. Huge.

No wonder he'd run today.

But he couldn't do it again. She knew he knew that, and somehow she was certain that there wouldn't be a repeat of today.

There was a steeliness to Marko—a sense that once he decided upon something he was unwavering in his determination to follow through. His successful military career reflected this. As did, Jas suspected, his extraordinary playboy reputation. As he'd told her today, once everyone—the media, Vela Ada, the world—had decided he was a player, he'd just run with it.

Her lips curved upwards; she didn't think doing so had been *entirely* a hardship for Marko.

However, after today, she was aware there was more to Marko than his reputation.

He was much more than just the Playboy Prince.

The next day, there were no royal engagements scheduled.

Jas, once again, had breakfast out on the terrace. However, today Marko didn't join her.

But, aside from an early morning run that Jas knew about only because two of her team had accompanied him, Marko didn't leave the palace all day.

Even so, Jas didn't lay eyes on him.

Instead, she spent the day working—not as a fake fiancée, but as the owner of a rapidly expanding personal protection services company. And after a day playing princess, she definitely had a lot to do.

Apart from remaining abreast of the two assignments her two other teams were currently engaged in, she also needed to plan ahead for Prince Marko. She might now be standing by his side in a different capacity, but she was still in charge of his protection. So her team needed to be out visiting upcoming venues, and liaising with Ivan and other palace staff about scheduling and logistics.

Frustratingly, Jas herself could no longer lead the scouting trips, although her team were more than capable of doing that without her. Even so, she asked for video footage to be taken where possible—even though she had each location's building plans, it wasn't quite the same as seeing a venue for herself.

In the evening, she ate dinner out on the terrace.

She told herself it was because the weather was glorious—warm with a breeze that carried the scent of conifers and just the slightest hint of the ocean—but when she found her gaze drifting to the French doors *once again*, she knew she was just lying to herself.

She had hoped Marko might join her.

Why?

As they'd driven home from the beach yesterday, Jas had barely spoken a word to Marko. If she'd expected becoming his unexpected confidante would lessen the constant tension between them, she'd been patently, spectacularly wrong.

His impromptu swim seemed to have washed away any chance of that happening. Back at the palace the Prince had excused himself to his rooms—and there he had remained.

Why was she surprised?

Because, really, wasn't it *normal* that things were a bit weird between them now? She'd gatecrashed an intensely private moment, and because of that—and *only* because of that—he'd been rawly honest with her. After all, why else would he tell her—effectively his employee—something so intensely personal?

Jas would bet her beloved vintage saucer collection that Marko wasn't one to confide in random strangers.

And that was who she was: a random stranger.

Just as he was a random stranger to her.

Who'd kissed her.

Who'd made her heart flip and every childhood fairy tale come true when he'd carried her in his arms.

Jasmine laid her knife and fork firmly on her dinner plate, loudly enough to make a noise and make the attentive wait person—*everyone* who worked in this palace was attentive—who'd just walked out the French doors startle.

The interruption as her plates were collected was timely.

It *did not matter* that Marko had kissed her—it hadn't been real. And it also *did not matter* that she thought about his lips on hers more often than she should—which was never—or about how being carried by someone so strong and powerful had taken her breath away.

Or that he'd asked her to come swimming with him in her underwear.

Jas squeezed her eyes tight.

Maybe he'd intended for her to swim in her dress. Or—more likely—because *he didn't think of her that way*, a nearly naked Jasmine Gallagher was of no concern to him.

Yes. That was definitely it.

Her phone rang, vibrating against her water glass.

Her mother.

Jasmine sighed.

She must have received her email, finally sent late the night before.

'You're actually marrying a *prince*?' her mum said, barely giving Jas an opportunity to say hello. 'This is not some elaborate April Fools type thing? I did not dream that my only daughter was on the front page of the *Canberra Herald*?'

'It's September, Mum,' Jas said, because it was the only thing she was actually allowed to refute.

'Jasmine Sadie Gallagher, this is *not* the time to be cute.'

'I know,' Jas said. 'I'm sorry, I don't know how to explain.'

That, at least, was honest.

Jas took a deep breath, and repeated what she'd written in her email. 'Marko asked me to keep this secret. He didn't want our relationship scrutinised by the media unless it went somewhere.'

'I'd say it's gone somewhere, Jas,' her mum said. 'And surely he would've understood that your own mother is an exception, and you could've said that I was trustworthy. It isn't like I would've told anyone, you must know that.'

The hurt was obvious in her mum's voice, and it made Jas feel ill. She couldn't remember lying to her mum since she was a teenager—and what she was lying about now was far more important than that one time she'd wagged school to go to the movies, and Jas *still* felt a little guilty about that.

'I'm sorry, Mum,' she said again. 'I really am.'

She couldn't wait until this charade was over and she could tell her the truth. No matter what her contract might say, she wasn't living the rest of her life with this lie hanging over the most important relationship in her life. Her family *was* just her and her mum. It always had been.

'So you'll be living there? In Vela Ada?'

Jas chewed her lip. 'I guess?'

'You *guess*? Isn't that the kind of thing you should discuss *before* you get engaged to royalty, Jasmine?'

This was horrendous. Guilt wrapped itself heavily around her shoulders.

'And, Jasmine, I was reading about this prince of yours, because I thought surely my daughter wouldn't marry a man who seems to have had sex with everything that walks in Europe—but, *no*, it is *that* prince. You know what he's called, right? The *Playboy* Prince? Why would you want to marry someone like that?'

Jas's head pounded with the effort to not blurt out everything.

Or to cry.

Her mum thought she was losing her daughter to the other side of the world to a man she didn't know, and none of that was true.

Right now, Jas genuinely hated herself for getting tangled up in this mess.

'He's not really like that, Mum. You can't believe everything you read in the tabloids.'

At least Jasmine believed that herself now. Marko was so much more.

'So all those photos with different women are what—all his closest friends?'

She knew her mum was just doing her job as a mother. She was supposed to be worried, she was supposed to be concerned—and yet Jas found herself snapping back at her.

'Actually,' she said firmly, 'most of those photos were taken years ago. More recently, Marko has rarely been photographed with women he's dating. The tabloids just like to reuse old photos, or make up stories with recent photos of him alone, particularly whenever he dares to go to the beach somewhere—and then speculate about who he might be dating. Just because an article says he dated someone, doesn't make it true.'

Last night, Jas had spent several hours discovering this all for herself.

Yes, Marko had probably deserved his playboy reputation, but the media were the ones who persisted with it—not Marko. But, Jas imagined, writing about how Prince Marko had settled down and now had a fiercely private personal life wouldn't sell many magazines, or get many clicks on social media.

There was a moment of silence, as if her mum was digesting this information.

'I'm sorry,' her mum said, eventually. 'I know you're no fool. You wouldn't be marrying him if he was really like that. I should've known. It's just that, after—'

Jas knew what was coming, and found herself gripping her phone so hard it hurt.

'—after what happened with Stuart, I can't help but worry about you.'

Now it was Jas's turn for a moment of silence.

'That was more than three years ago, Mum,' she said, doing her best to sound perfectly calm. 'It's not an issue any more.'

'But what he did...' The anger in Jas's mum's voice was familiar, and very real. 'After something like that, I'd hate you to trust the wrong man again.'

Jas shook her head, even without her mother there to see it. 'That *won't* happen again, Mum. It hasn't. Marko isn't the wrong man.' She swallowed. 'He's the right man. You don't have to worry.'

'Have you told him about Stuart?'

Jas had to hold back a hysterical burst of laugher. *Tell Prince Marko?*

For a crazy, maniacal second, she imagined quietly sitting down with Marko and explaining in a matter-of-fact tone exactly what Stuart had done. And what she'd done, just before Stuart had so irretrievably shattered her trust, in her misguided, desperate act of supposed love…

'Of course I've told him,' Jas said, with calmness that she certainly did not feel. 'We're engaged.'

'How did he—?'

'Mum,' she said firmly. 'Please. I don't want to talk about it.'

Thankfully her mum let it go. For now, at least.

But how *would* Marko respond?

It was the most rhetorical of questions. She'd *never* tell him.

She could probably guess, though. He'd respond like every other person who knew: *Jas, what were you thinking?*

Of course, everyone hated Stuart too, but they still asked the question. And really, once they asked that, all their vitriol directed at her ex became irrelevant.

Because it was their judgment that she remembered. That she felt—still—deep inside her.

Marko wouldn't be any different.

Wouldn't he?

Jas shoved that question out of her mind.

Her mum spoke for a few more minutes, but

Jas remembered none of it when she eventually hung up.

Instead, she sat back in her chair, and stared out across the trees and out to the city of Vela Ada—now identifiable only by a mass of lights, with the day shifting into darkness as they'd talked.

He's the right man.

Well, that certainly wasn't true—at least, not outside this charade. That right man for her might, in fact, not even exist. In the past few years since Stuart, Jas had begun to wonder if there were *any* right men, for anyone. If love, and especially the concept of *one true love*, might not be an actual attainable thing.

After all, she'd loved Stuart.

Or thought she had.

A French door opened, and someone, somewhere, turned on the fairy lights that must decorate every outside space at the palace.

It was Marko who had stepped outside.

But as he did Jasmine pushed back her seat, and got to her feet.

'I'm sorry,' she said. 'I was just going to my room.'

She managed a smile as she walked past him, but that was all she could manage.

She couldn't remain out here, in the aftermath of

lying to her mother and the unwanted reminder of her disastrous recent history with men, and simply talk to Marko.

So she didn't.

It was for the best, this new understanding between Jas and Marko.

It was an unspoken understanding, but in the almost week since he'd invited Jas to swim with him, it would appear they'd both separately come to the same conclusion.

This was strictly a professional arrangement.

No more friendly banter—unless they were being observed, of course. No more flirting. And *definitely* no more deeply personal revelations.

What had come over him, on that beach, to tell Jasmine so much?

He'd never spoken of his past, or of his father, to any woman. To anyone. Once he'd used to share most things with his brother, but those days had long passed, even before Lukas's coronation.

So to confide in Jas was definitely out of character.

That had made him feel…not exactly uncomfortable around her, but it had certainly added another layer to the tension already between them.

Despite Jas's no-kissing clause, the hum of attraction had not suddenly ceased to exist. It certainly hadn't gone anywhere when he'd so impulsively invited her into the ocean, and it persisted now, despite their carefully strict professionalism.

And it was amongst this attraction that there was now this added tension: Jasmine knew something about him that no one else did.

He *hated* that.

Today he was with Jas at a morning tea for a charity for which Lukas was patron.

It was a relatively small event, held at a hall in the city, which Lukas attended with Petra each year.

Consequently, they'd been greeted by waiting media as they'd exited their car.

Which Marko had handled with no problems at all.

As he'd handled every interaction he'd had with the media since that damn, stupid escape from that school.

Because he'd needed to. Now was not the time to be so self-indulgent. Of course, he still hated the media intensely—it was just now he was bothering to hide it.

He was *not* going to give anyone a headline that would worry Lukas. Instead, he would be the dutiful Prince that Lukas needed him to be, and smile, and nod, and answer—or deflect—inane questions.

It wasn't easy for Marko, but it was getting easier, one plastic smile at a time.

Currently, his plastic smile was aching with overuse, as he and Jas wrapped up their latest conversation. Alone, just briefly, before Ivan subtly brought the next group over. It was constant at these events—a steady stream of people and questions and politeness, carefully managed so that he and Jas could meet as many guests as possible.

There was a soft *clink* as Jas replaced her teacup on the delicate saucer she held. The sound drew his attention—and just briefly Jas met his gaze, and smiled.

'I don't know how Lukas and Petra do this,' she said. 'One week of it and I'm already exhausted.'

Marko nodded. This was their third event for the week—not including her welcome ball. The school visit, an art gallery opening, and now this charity function. 'He's very stoic, my brother,' he said. 'And also just genuinely interested in everyone. He could extract the life story from a lamp post, and find it fascinating.'

Jas laughed. 'You aren't using lamp posts as a metaphor for the people of Vela Ada, are you, Marko?'

'No!' Marko said. 'If anything, I'm the lamp post. And also not very good at asking leading questions.'

'So you're a taciturn lamp post,' she teased, tilting her head as she studied him. 'Interesting.'

Her eyes sparkled with humour.

'You know,' he said, 'this *isn't* actually the most ridiculous conversation I've had today.'

Jas grinned. 'I know. *Are* you going to be guest judge at the Vela Ada National Dog Show?'

'I expect so,' Marko said drily, 'seeing as detailing my lack of qualifications wasn't much of a deterrent. And how about you—will you ensure I never stray by baking Baba Lucija's *madjarica* cake for me every Sunday?'

'No,' Jas said firmly. 'Although the recipe looked good, so I'm going to keep it.'

Ivan was approaching with the next small group.

Jas took another sip of her tea, and then leaned close to Marko, standing on her tiptoes so only he could hear her.

'You're good at this,' she said, firmly. 'Nothing lamp-post-like about you, I promise.' He looked down to meet her gaze, surprised.

Jas narrowed her eyes, as if considering something.

'Well, maybe you could smile a bit more.'

'More!' he whispered, disbelieving. But Jas gave nothing away as to if she was teasing, or genuine—as surely it was physically impossible for him to smile *more*? Jasmine simply smiled at him, serenely.

And so Marko, of course, found himself smiling too—and this time, as he was introduced to their latest guests, it was a smile without the faintest hint of plastic.

It had been nice to make Marko laugh.

She'd tried, for a whole week, to be strictly professional, but she was just spending too much time with the Prince to maintain it. So after the lamppost incident, she began to relax a little around Marko again—chatting with him in the car on the way to events, and talking more freely at the events themselves.

But outside the royal events they attended—and in the second week there were only two—Jas backed off again. Even when they met for a meal—and they were scheduled to have at least one together each day as part of their ruse—Jas didn't encourage much conversation.

It was just easier that way.

No confusion, no chance she'd misinterpret Marko's innate, rather smouldering charisma as having anything to do with her specifically. They were just two people working together. Professionally.

So they would eat breakfast, or lunch, or dinner—usually out on the terrace—in a not quite comfortable almost silence. Marko began bringing along whatever book he was reading—generally autobiographies or science fiction—while Jas would manage Gallagher Personal Protection Services.

Which didn't mean that at times Jas didn't want to ask him questions. About what it was like growing up in this palace—and *why* he'd hated it so. About his obviously complex relationship with his brother. About all sorts of things.

But she never asked, of course. Because it was none of her business.

Midway through Jas's third week as fake fiancée, they headed for Vela Ada harbour for a sailing regatta. Terraced houses huddled close to the water, overlooking everything from rowboats to yachts, all moored along narrow jetties, bobbing gently in the undulating sea. Crowds milled near the water's edge, kids dangled their legs into the water, and couples drank dark coffee in cafés. When they'd arrived, there'd been a large crowd waiting for them, but now they'd finished an extended meet and greet the crowd had dispersed somewhat, and they were being led to their exclusive VIP marquee.

It was a beautiful day, the sun warm on Jas's shoulders, revealed by the drop sleeves of her white summery dress. The novelty of the beautiful clothes she got to wear still hadn't worn off, and Jas had never felt more sophisticated than she did right now in her wide-brimmed, fashionably floppy hat and dark, oversized sunglasses.

She also still felt like a total fraud, but, miraculously, now three weeks in, the people of Vela Ada continued to embrace her as their future princess. Three weeks of shaking hands, and small talk, and smiling—and countless newspaper and magazine articles—and Marko's plan continued to go to plan. Everyone actually believed she was Marko's fiancée.

It was crazy, really.

Although the real reason anyone believed any of this was because of Marko.

In public, he played the affectionate fiancé in the most natural, casual ways: he took every opportunity to hold her hand, he was forever touching her—the small of her back, her shoulder…

And the way he *spoke* to her. And about her…

It was beautiful.

It made her *feel* beautiful.

And in those moments, a part of Jasmine let herself believe it was all real.

Only a very small part, the part of her that in the dead of night couldn't remember why their no-kissing clause had seemed so essential—but a part of her, nonetheless.

She'd seen that part of her in some of the many photographs taken of her. She tried to avoid paying attention to them, because—unfortunately—becoming a fake princess-to-be had not suddenly made her effortlessly photogenic. But she was human, and so she'd looked herself up on the Internet. And amongst the photos that made her cringe at her awkward expression or an unflattering angle (Marko, without exception, always looked devastatingly handsome) there had been images of her simply looking at Marko. And in those images it was easy to see why Vela Ada—and the world—thought they were in love.

Because her gaze was that of a woman besotted.

It had scared her at first—her mother's warning warring with her own determination to never be so romantically stupid again—but then she'd started paying attention to Marko's gaze in those photos.

And his—while not besotted—told its own story. His gaze was that of a man with all sorts of delicious plans for the woman he was looking at. A gaze that made her shiver.

It was also a gaze that was absent the moment they left the public eye.

At the palace, there were two people with a business arrangement and a no-kissing clause.

So, they were *both* pretending. They *both* could separate fact from fiction.

Marko's wrist bumped against hers as they walked along the marina, and then—in an action that was now so familiar—he laced his fingers with hers.

In a reaction that was also familiar, Jas's belly flipped over, and electricity zipped up her arm.

But she ignored all that, and, because it was her job too, she looked up at Marko and smiled.

Her eyes were hidden behind her dark glasses, but his weren't.

And when he smiled back at her, and squeezed her hand, looking at her as if she were the only woman for him in the world…

She simply acknowledged, once again, what a remarkably good actor he was.

CHAPTER NINE

JASMINE MIGHT THINK he was good at this—at mingling with all these total strangers beneath an open-sided marquee where waiters constantly circulated with obscenely expensive champagne—but Marko did not feel that way at all.

He was getting more practised, certainly. He now didn't feel he needed to wrack his brain for things to say, and instead he found words and platitudes spilling easily from his mouth. The people he met—and honestly, most were really very nice people—seemed happy enough, anyway.

Obviously he was no Lukas, but then, he wasn't trying to be. He was playing a role for a defined period of time, and the people of Vela Ada seemed okay with that. He had no doubt that Jasmine was having a huge influence on his acceptance into this role, and that having her by his side was the reason why he was attracting crowds that rivalled the King and Queen's at events. Without Jasmine, he was simply the absent, disreputable Prince, but

with her, he was—according to the headlines—
a changed man. A changed man who had come
home to Vela Ada.

Home?

No. Vela Ada wasn't his home. But this perception fed perfectly into the narrative that he and
Jasmine had created, and for that he was grateful.

He'd spoken to Lukas earlier this morning, just
before his brother had begun his day of chemotherapy. He was doing as well as could be expected,
he'd said. And he'd asked about Jas.

So, everyone believed in his relationship with
Jas.

This was good, right? Exactly what he'd wanted?

'Your Highness?'

Marko blinked. The older couple standing in
front of him were looking at him curiously.

See? This was why he was no good at this. He'd
just completely checked out of this conversation.

He took a long sip of his champagne, and glanced
at Jas.

He'd meant to shoot her a look of thanks for carrying the conversation, but then he noticed the way
her lips were arranged in a tense, straight line.

'We were just discussing how lovely it is that
you've settled down,' the older man said. Marko
glanced at the name tag pinned to the lapel of his

suit jacket. He didn't recognise the name, but the seafood business printed in italics beneath it, he did. The largest in the country.

Marko nodded without a lot of commitment, wondering what he'd missed. He could sense the tension in Jas, despite the gap between them.

'Yes,' said the woman. She was beautiful, with white-blonde hair wrapped into a polished chignon. 'And to choose such a *successful* woman. How nice.'

'I'm very proud of Jas's achievements,' Marko said, but a little warily now. 'She is exceptional at what she does.'

There was a glint to the woman's gaze when she looked at Jas that Marko did not like.

'But it must have been hard giving up your old lifestyle,' the man said.

'I haven't left the military,' Marko said. 'I'm not sure what you mean.'

But he did, of course. The surname on their name tags suddenly clicked into place, and a half-formed memory of a young woman with hair the same colour as in that chignon.

He turned to Jas, taking her hand. He lifted his gaze in search of Ivan, to signal that this conversation was over.

But the older couple weren't paying attention, seemingly intent on delivering their message.

'So many *beautiful* women,' he said, in a chummy, 'just between us men' type tone. 'Models, actresses, the most stunning women in Vela Ada. And with all that choice, you chose Jasmine.'

He smiled at Jas in a way that made Marko feel violent.

'You *must* be very proud of her,' the woman said. 'Of all that she's *achieved*. Because, well—'

The woman whipped her hand in front of her mouth, and laughed, as if she'd accidentally let something slip, instead of carefully constructing this entire conversation.

Jas gripped his hand tightly, but she murmured, 'It's okay. I'm fine.'

But this really wasn't fine. Anger bubbled inside him, and the urge to tell these people exactly what he thought of them—and loudly—was almost impossible to resist.

Yet resist it he did.

Because if he didn't, if he made a scene, it would be in the papers, it would be all over the Internet. And he suspected that was exactly what this couple wanted.

So instead, he faced them both again.

'Jas is the most remarkable woman I've ever

met,' he said, in a deliberately calm and low tone. 'Now, if you'll excuse me, I—'

The man's words were muttered beneath his breath, but neither Marko nor Jas misheard: *It'll never last.*

'Ivan,' Marko said, more loudly now. His valet stepped closer. 'Please escort this couple to the exit.'

He didn't bother to provide a reason. He just wanted them gone.

In fact, he also wanted to be gone. From this marquee, from all these people, and from anyone who had an opinion on him, or Jas, or their relationship.

'Want to come for a walk?' he asked Jas.

They didn't leave in a hurry. Instead, Marko politely made his way through the crowd, explaining that he wanted to show Jasmine *Mjesto za Ljubljenje.*

Everyone smiled when Marko said that, although Jas had no idea why, her efforts at learning basic Slavic phrases not having extended to those words. *Za* might mean 'of'? She couldn't remember.

'Where are we going?' Jas asked—partly because she was curious, but mostly because Marko couldn't just walk off into the distance. Her team still had a job to do.

'*Mjesto za Ljubljenje* is up there—' Marko gestured to where the harbour curved and merged into a rocky beach. 'On the other side of those trees.'

'That's still part of the exclusion zone,' Jas said, referring to the area surrounding the marquee that had been cleared for anyone but guests. Palace security patrolled the edges of the zone, ensuring the privacy and security of the Prince—and mostly to keep the paparazzi at bay.

'Exactly,' Marko said. He turned to Scott and Simon, who had materialised at their sides. 'So, guys—could you keep your distance?'

Marko needed some space; it was obvious to Jasmine in every tense line of his body. *She* needed some space, actually.

Which was silly. Because as much as she appreciated Marko's defence of her, and as much as she acknowledged that such rudeness towards anyone—let alone your country's Prince and his fiancée—was utterly outrageous...

That couple had been right.

Marko would *never* have chosen her, from all the women he'd had to choose from—and who he would have to choose from again, once this was over—based on her looks.

To have it so baldly stated was definitely a direct hit to her vanity.

But in reality…it didn't actually matter.

He hadn't chosen her—for any reason—and he never would.

So, alone, Jas and Marko went for a walk.

He still held her hand, although it was obviously for show—given they remained in full view of the marquee.

He didn't say a word, he simply walked briskly, his gaze straight ahead.

He only paused—and dropped her hand—when they passed the last mooring to reach the edge of the marina, and Jas needed to stop to take off her heels. Marko removed his shoes too.

They now walked along the sandy beach of a narrow point that stretched out from the town. With no buildings and covered in a mix of tall trees and scrubby plants, it was a stark contrast to the bustling crowd behind them. But Jas still sensed she was being watched, and it wasn't until they'd rounded the top of the point—and were hidden from view—that she began to relax.

'It's all national park here,' Marko said suddenly. 'It extends along the coast for a few kilometres. There are walking trails, some picnic spots and a few lookouts, but not much else.'

'It's beautiful,' Jas said. And it was. Their only company was the ocean, and the white yachts that dotted it as they took part in the regatta Jas had almost forgotten about. 'It's hard to believe we're so close to the city.'

He was still walking. A bit faster now, so Jas had to lengthen her own stride to keep up.

'I'm very sorry about before,' he said. 'I think they must be the parents of a woman I dated briefly. Seems they maybe had hopes of marrying into royalty.'

Jas shrugged. 'It's okay.'

Marko stopped. The beach had narrowed here, and water lapped almost against their toes.

'It's not okay,' he said, facing Jas. It was mid-afternoon and the sun made him squint.

The sea breeze had loosened Jasmine's hair from its bun, her hair no longer contained by the hat she'd forgotten back at the marquee.

'No, really,' Jas said, 'it is. You must get so frustrated with how everyone refers to your past. That guy made it sound like—'

'No, Jas,' he said, interrupting. 'Don't make this about me. They were very offensive towards *you*.'

Jas crossed her arms in front of herself. 'So they were mean to me.' She shrugged again. 'So what? I'm pretty tough, remember?'

She raised her eyebrows and smiled, but Marko was refusing to play along.

'It wasn't acceptable,' he insisted.

Jas wrinkled her forehead, confused. Why was he so stuck on this? 'Thank you very much for your chivalry back there, but, please—don't worry about it. I'm really fine. Besides—'

But then she snapped her mouth shut.

'Besides what?'

Now it was Jas's turn to start walking, and she did so with big, urgent strides. Did they really need to have a conversation about how much less attractive she was than all his *real* past partners?

'It doesn't matter.'

He caught up with her effortlessly, and they walked together, gentle waves occasionally covering their feet, the water cool against her skin.

'You told me, that first night, that you don't look anything like the women I date,' he said shrewdly. 'You don't still believe that, surely?'

'It really doesn't matter what I think,' Jas pointed out. 'Everyone else seems to believe it's plausible we're engaged—except this couple today—and that's what's important.'

'I disagree,' he said.

'With what? That everyone believes we're really engaged? Or that it's not important they do?'

She was being deliberately obtuse, not understanding why Marko wanted to have this conversation.

'I disagree that you don't look like a woman I'd date,' he said.

He stepped in front of her, forcing her to stop.

Jas made herself look up at him, and tucked long escaped strands of her hair roughly behind her ears.

'That's very kind of you to tell me that,' she said neutrally. 'And trust me, I think I have relatively good self-esteem—but I'm not delusional, Marko. I'm no supermodel. Heck, I wasn't close to being the most beautiful girl in my year at school—or probably even in my *street*—let alone the most beautiful woman in Vela Ada. That couple kind of had a point. If you were, in fact, *actually* engaged to me, it *wouldn't* be for my looks.' She grinned now. 'It would definitely be my sparkling personality that won you over.'

But Marko wasn't smiling.

'Do you really think so little of me that you think looks are all I care about?'

'No,' Jas said. 'It's just—'

'Based on what you've read in magazines and photos you've seen, you know what kind of man I am? Just like that couple thought they knew me?'

He swallowed. 'Despite the amount of time we've spent together, that's *still* the man you think I am? Despite what I've—'

He stopped abruptly.

Despite what I've told you. Jas *knew* that was what he'd been about to say.

But he wouldn't say it. Jas also knew that Marko still hated what he'd revealed to her on that beach.

Jas shook her head. *'No,'* she said.

But, she realised, even though she'd defended him to her mother, part of her, maybe, still labelled him as the Playboy Prince.

'Okay,' she said. 'I'm sorry. I probably have made unfair assumptions. But why are we even having this conversation? It doesn't matter if it's my looks or my personality or whatever that you're attracted to, because *you're not* attracted to me. Remember? This isn't real.'

Jasmine stepped around Marko, and continued down the beach.

She hugged herself as she walked, unsure why she felt so agitated, and frustrated that her cheeks had definitely heated into a telling blush.

She was *just* working with Marko. None of this mattered.

It was only her ego that was bruised, not her heart…

Her heart?

Ha! She couldn't help but smile. Now she *was* being delusional. Sure, Marko was very handsome. And charming. And, it turned out, smart, and complex, and thoughtful, and he laughed at her jokes...

But she'd always known that he wasn't really interested in her. He'd flirted with her, maybe. Checked her out, that first time they'd met...but— that was what he *did*. Right?

Because he was the Playboy Prince...

Except, he wasn't. Not really. She knew that.

She shook her head, as if trying to shake these unwanted thoughts free.

No. He might make her tummy flip over, and her skin tingle—but that didn't mean there was anything more there. She was only human, and he *was* gorgeous. But she knew that was all it was— an attraction she was very capable of controlling. A physical attraction, nothing more.

The beach sand had merged into rocks—large and flat, and arranged like a natural, gradual staircase. Jasmine made her way up them, her strappy sandals still in one hand. She didn't look back, but she knew Marko was behind her.

At the top was a large, flat space, paved in small square cobblestones in differing shades of cream. At the centre a line of dark grey stones formed a square, and inside that even smaller pavers formed the words *Mjesto za Ljubljenje.*

It seemed she had found Marko's destination.

Jas stepped into the square—it felt as if that was what she was supposed to do—and let her sandals drop to the ground.

It must be a lookout point, Jas decided. The view was certainly spectacular—from here she could look back towards the city of Vela Ada, its red-roofed buildings peeking out beyond the trees of the national park as they covered the undulating hills. And ahead of her was the ocean, a sparkling, perfect azure, the horizon only interrupted by yachts and foaming waves.

Marko stepped into the square.

Suddenly, with Marko beside her, the square seemed tiny—barely big enough for the two of them, their feet covering most of the writing.

'What does it mean?' Jas asked. She attempted to pronounce it. *'Mjesto za Ljubljenje.'*

'I worked out why we're having this conversation,' Marko said, ignoring her current question to reference a question she hadn't really wanted him to answer. 'Why what that couple said bothered me so much, and why I don't like you being so okay with it.'

They both kept staring out to the ocean, not looking at each other, and not touching.

Jas hated how she was feeling right now, an unfamiliar mix of embarrassment and hurt that she knew was misplaced. Why wouldn't Marko just move on from this? She wasn't fragile; she didn't need him to try and make her feel better.

'It's because I didn't like those people saying you weren't beautiful, and I don't like that you think you aren't.'

Jas rolled her eyes, turning to look up at him now. 'Seriously, Marko, there is a *lot* more to me than how I look. I'm genuinely, totally fine. You don't have to say nice things to make me feel good about myself.'

'I'm not saying it to make you feel better. And I know there is so much more to you than your appearance—I know there is so much more to everyone than their appearance. But—the thing is, I particularly like your appearance, and it turns out it's important to me that you know that.'

'You *particularly like my appearance*?' Jas said, her lips quirking upwards. 'Well, that's a new one. I'll file that compliment beside the *Well Done for Trying* stickers I got as a kid, or that one time I received a "sound" rating in a performance review from a sergeant who really didn't like me. What does "sound" even mean in that cont—?'

'Jasmine,' Marko said, cutting off her stream of words. 'Stop. I'm trying to tell you I think you're beautiful, and you're too busy being facetious to listen.'

'I wasn't being—' she argued, automatically. And then stopped. 'Pardon me?'

'I said I think you're beautiful. Really beautiful, actually. And I *am* attracted to you. Very much so.'

'But—'

'I'm actually a bit confused why you would ever think I *wasn't*. You knew I checked you out that first time we met. You knew I liked kissing you, and was angling to kiss you again later that night. And you knew I invited you to swim with me that day, and, believe me, my dreams have done their best to imagine how you would've looked in your underwear if you'd said yes. In your wet underwear, actually.'

Oh, God. Marko's deep, delicious voice sent shivers down her spine.

She closed her eyes, and took a long, deep breath.

'But since that day at the beach, you've been so different when we've been alone. You've kept your distance,' she said.

'So have you,' Marko pointed out.

'I was being professional.'

'So was I,' he said. 'But I was putting aside the attraction between us. I certainly wasn't pretending it didn't exist.'

'I haven't been pretending!' Jas said, narrowing her gaze. 'I'm just not as arrogant as you, assuming that every person I meet is melting into a puddle of lust in my presence. *You* don't even know if I'm into you. Maybe I'm not.'

He just looked at her steadily, with infuriating self-assurance in his gaze.

'Maybe you weren't pretending,' Marko continued now, his voice low. 'Maybe it was just plain old denial. Because, surely, you feel this too.'

He reached out, taking her right hand, and lifting it to his chest. Jas stretched her fingers out, until her palm was flat against his heart.

'Can you feel that?' he asked hoarsely.

His heart beat like a drum beneath her touch.

Jas wasn't capable of doing much more than nod, and so that was what she did.

Then Marko's fingers curved around her wrist to press gently against her skin—against her own pulse, a pulse that beat every bit as rapidly as his heart.

She watched as Marko's lips curved into a knowing smile, but then her gaze met his, and all she could concentrate on were his eyes. Eyes that were hot with want—for *her*.

But, Jas realised only now, that wasn't a complete surprise. Since the moment they'd met, electricity had sparked between them, and that connection had only grown since then with every touch, every word, and every laugh.

So he'd been right, she had been denying this, for reasons beyond professionalism. For such professionalism didn't require denial, it simply required restraint.

She didn't *want* to want Marko, because Marko was not the right man for her. Even now, as she stood within the spell of his words and his proximity, she knew he was not the man who would mend her still-broken heart, or who she could trust to never hurt her. Because Marko, while not exactly the playboy he was portrayed as, was also not going to fall in love with Jasmine Gallagher from Canberra. In just over two months' time he would return to his military career, and to a world that would not involve her.

Of that she had no doubt.

'Marko,' Jas said, attempting to sound serious, but ending up soft and breathy. 'As it appears we both have thrown professionalism out the window, can I just confirm something?'

'Anything,' he murmured.

He was brushing his thumb against the sensitive skin of her wrist, making it nearly impossible for Jas to think aside from wondering how something so simple could make her knees feel so weak.

'Uh—' she began, then swallowed. Straightened her shoulders. 'This is important,' she said—partly as a reminder to herself. 'I just want to be clear what this is. So if we tear up the no-kissing clause, we'll be *not* not kissing for how long, exactly?'

Marko raised his eyebrows. 'I don't think it's necessary to update our contract, Jas.'

'But not beyond these three months together, right?'

The look of horror in Marko's gaze told Jas everything she needed to know. It also made her laugh out loud.

'Wow, Marko—way to freak out,' Jas said. 'Don't panic, I'm thinking something fun and easy too. I'm on the same page.'

And she most definitely was. Especially now there was *no* danger she might start imagining a future for them that would never be.

Marko seemed to have decided he'd had enough of talking. He stepped closer, almost sandwiching their hands between them—but not quite. Still, they only touched above his heartbeat, while the ocean breeze tangled her skirt against his legs.

'*Mjesto za Ljubljenje,*' he said, now so close she had to tilt her chin up to meet his gaze. 'You asked before what it means.'

Jas curled her toes against the smooth shape of those words against her feet, and nodded, although right now all she cared about was getting closer to Marko.

'It translates to Place of Love,' he said, in a rough tone that did delicious things to Jas's insides. 'But in English, people usually call these places a kissing spot—which is what it's intended to be.'

'There's more than one?' Jas asked, her gaze travelling downwards to his lips.

'Mmm-hmm,' Marko said. 'Across the island, and also throughout Croatia. One of many ideas we've borrowed from our neighbour.'

'An *excellent* idea,' Jas said firmly. But she was getting impatient now. What was Marko waiting for?

His lips—the lips she couldn't drag her gaze away from—had formed into a smile. God, he *knew* what he was doing to her. But, with her hand against his heart, she also knew *exactly* what she was doing to him.

He was just as affected by her nearness as she

was by his. And with that knowledge came power. And with the clarity of expectation they both now had—came freedom.

Suddenly she remembered something: whispered words from a night that seemed a lifetime ago.

She stood, on tiptoes, to speak almost against his lips. 'Can I kiss you?' she said, repurposing Marko's own words.

'You, Jasmine Gallagher, can do anything you want.'

And so Jas was smiling as she bridged the tiniest of gaps between them to press her mouth against his.

At first, their kiss had many similarities to that one in front of the glitterati of Vela Ada. His lips were warm, and tasted of just a hint of the salty breeze—and remained closed. As if he was waiting for her.

Like then, they were joined only by their hands and lips, and like then, it was incredibly, impossibly sexy.

A kiss that promised *so* much more, and now—now there was no question that there was definitely so much more to come.

But it was as if because of that knowledge they'd both decided to build the anticipation, to wait just that little bit longer. To allow the heat that had already built between them to keep on building until every fibre of their bodies felt engulfed in flames.

And so, when Jasmine's lips finally opened against Marko's, and he brushed his tongue against hers, the sensation was so incredible, so overwhelming, that Jas—strong, capable, always together Jas—felt her knees give way.

But she fell no further than into Marko's arms— that were there so quickly it was as if he knew what would happen, or maybe he had fallen into her as well.

It didn't matter; all Jas knew now was that her hands were twined behind Marko's neck and his hands were at her waist and back, pressing her close against him.

To be *held* against Marko was just something else entirely. After weeks of sparks from simply holding hands to now have his chest, his hips, his thighs pressed hard against hers was enough to make Jas sure she would ignite.

Or combust into that puddle of lust she'd teased Marko about but had always been revealingly close to the truth.

Marko did something to her in a way that she'd never experienced before.

It had her believing in things she had no place

believing: that love and happy ever afters were actually possible.

Although—obviously—not with Marko.

She moved her mouth from Marko's, to take a deep breath and try and right her rioting, silly thoughts. But Marko only took the opportunity to press kisses against her jaw, working his way to the sensitive skin of her neck and below her ear.

He murmured something against her skin, foreign words that could have meant anything, but still practically made her swoon.

This was *not* the time for thinking, it was for *feeling*, and so Jas simply closed her eyes and let sensation take over.

Her own hands traced patterns against his neck and shoulders, and brushed through his army-short hair. She worked one hand back to his front, in an attempt to undo his tie in a quest to touch more of his skin—but she soon gave up and simply slid a button undone. Then two.

Marko's hands were searching for bare skin too, one making its way to her bare shoulders, his fingers sliding just slightly beneath the fabric below her shoulder blades.

Then he was kissing her mouth again, and if the kiss had begun as Jasmine's it was now all Marko's as he kissed her thoroughly with lips and tongue—

at times teasing her with his mouth, or allowing her to tease him—and then he'd take control in a way that made Jas lose sense of anything. When she was lost within his kiss.

Eventually, Jas—or Marko, she had no idea—broke their lips apart, and they stood, foreheads still touching, as they each took deep, harsh breaths.

'Do we need to go back to the marquee?' Jas asked when she was again capable of speaking.

'Probably,' Marko said, but his smile was wicked. 'Lukas definitely would.'

'Are we?' Jas prompted.

Marko took a step back, and his gaze travelled across Jasmine—with now familiar heat in it—from her eyes, to her lips, then down to the askew bodice of her dress and her breasts that still rose and fell rapidly.

Jas took Marko in too—his own heavy breathing, that gorgeous olive skin she could see where she'd so artlessly yanked his shirt open…and the promises in his piercing blue gaze.

'We're not going back to the marquee,' Jas said.

'No,' Marko agreed, lacing his fingers with hers as he led her back down the rocky steps. 'We—most definitely—are not.'

CHAPTER TEN

HE'D NEVER SLEPT with a woman in the palace.

This realisation—in both senses of the word—came to Marko as the dawn crept its way around the edges of his curtains.

Although, he wasn't so much looking at his curtains as looking at Jasmine—her shape revealed in increasingly more satisfying detail as the morning light gradually entered his suite.

She lay, fast asleep, naked, beside him. She had her back to him, his sheets caught up around her waist, but leaving her back bare. While he'd been contemplating the realisation that Jas was the only woman who'd lain beside him here, he'd only been able to see as much as the darkness would allow: not much more than her silhouette, her hair a dark wave against the crisp whiteness of her pillow.

But now, he could appreciate the pale alabaster of her skin, and the gentle curve of her spine. He could recognise the smattering of freckles he'd discovered last night on her shoulders, and he could be grateful that his sheets did not hide the smooth roundness of her bottom.

And he could also wonder at how he felt, having a woman here. In the palace. With him.

Last night, it hadn't even been a consideration. *Nothing* had been more important than returning home, and kissing Jasmine again. And again.

It also would've been ridiculous to go anywhere else.

They were supposedly engaged. To take her to a hotel would've been ludicrous, if it had even occurred to him.

But it hadn't. So here he was, with a woman in his room.

He supposed, up until now, bringing a woman into the palace had never been a possibility. The palace wasn't the place to bring a one-night stand—and yes, at one stage, he'd had his fair share of those—but it equally wasn't the place to bring any woman he'd been seeing.

To do so would imply too much—it would imply a relationship, and a relationship was something he'd never had.

But even if he had—if something had stretched from weeks to months with a woman—the palace was not the place he would've wanted to take her.

This place, to Marko, was a place of suffocation.

And of scrutiny and surveillance. Here he was controlled by the expectations of his birth, of his family, his brother—and of everyone in Vela Ada.

Here there was no pretending that he wasn't a prince. Here it was *all* he was.

He'd never wanted to bring a woman into that. To put her through that.

Yet, despite all that—here Jas was. In the palace, and in his bed.

So—how did he feel about it?

Not great.

But also—not entirely bad.

Not even close to bad, actually.

His unease at the situation was more an itchiness in his subconscious—an awareness that he should be feeling regret right now.

Yet he didn't. He wouldn't say he felt comfortable, exactly. But equally, he didn't want Jas to leave his bed any time soon.

The realisation surprised him, but, as he watched Jasmine roll onto her back, still asleep, one arm out-flung and now almost touching his shoulder, it probably shouldn't.

It was because Jasmine had come to his room with no expectations.

In her typical way she hadn't even allowed him to kiss her without determining exactly what she was getting into—much like the way she had her team scout out venues before events. Jas was *always* prepared in her professional career—and it would seem she approached her personal life in the same way.

Marko smiled as he reached that conclusion.

Jas made him smile a lot, he'd discovered. When they'd both backed off after his accidental divulgement at that private beach, it had felt like the right decision. But within days he'd missed the way she teased him, and her willingness to say whatever popped into her head.

Fortunately, it hadn't lasted long, and he supposed he should've realised he and Jas were always heading in this direction, and into bed. Right from the start he'd been drawn to her, he just hadn't realised how strongly until meeting that silly couple with their misplaced jealousy.

Although, that wasn't entirely true.

He'd known how strongly he was drawn to Jasmine from the moment he'd kissed her that very first evening. He'd just, as he'd told Jas, not pursued it.

Jas had been right to keep things professional between them. And he'd needed to minimise any complications amidst this exceedingly complicated deception. He couldn't risk anything going wrong, because he needed to keep everything together for Lukas.

But yesterday...

Suddenly, he hadn't been able to pretend any more.

And because of Jasmine—because of who she was—so straightforward, so structured—he *knew* she had no expectations beyond right now. Whether it led to tomorrow, or a week, or the rest of their three-month contract—it *would* end eventually. Jas was not imagining herself as a future princess, and as such there was no significance in her lying here beside him right now.

None.

So that must be why he felt fine.

Actually—as Jas's eyes fluttered open and her lips formed into a sleepy, sexy good-morning smile—he changed his mind.

Right now—as he leant forward to kiss the beautiful, naked woman in his bed—he felt pretty damn fantastic.

Given the nature of Jas's career, she'd never been particularly active on social media. You never knew how a person with nefarious intentions might track or monitor a client she was looking after, so it wasn't as if she could ever post a selfie of herself at work or anything. Nevertheless, she did have social media accounts, even though she'd been ignoring the hundreds of messages she'd received since the news of her 'engagement' had become news across the world.

Soon after she and Marko eventually emerged from his suite for an extremely late breakfast on the terrace, Marko had been called away for something royal-related by Ivan, and while she'd waited for him to return she'd logged into her account on her phone.

Slowly she weeded through her messages—ignoring those from people she didn't know at all, and also those from friends of the 'we went to kindergarten together but I probably wouldn't recognise you in the local supermarket' variety.

To the rest—some of her friends from the police academy, and the small group of women she'd gone to high school with that she still always made sure to catch up with when in Canberra—she sent short messages that didn't invite extended conversation.

Yes, I'm really engaged to a prince. I'm sorry we had to keep it secret until now, I hope you understand. Don't worry—I'll tell you all the details when I'm next home.

And by then, of course, it would all be over.

Jas still didn't feel okay about lying to her friends, but for some reason, now, it didn't feel so impossible.

Maybe it didn't feel so much of a lie now that she had *some* form of relationship with Marko? Other than a business relationship, of course.

Jas smiled. Yup, it was definitely more than a business relationship, now.

To wake up this morning the way she had—with Marko there, simply looking at her, with the *most* remarkable expression in his eyes… And then…

Well.

It had been pretty damn spectacular.

Jas looked up from her phone at the sound of Marko's footsteps. It was a little cooler today, and he wore jeans and a faded T-shirt. He hadn't bothered to shave that morning, and Jas thought the shadow of stubble across his jaw made him even more impossibly handsome. Like a slightly more dangerous version of Prince Marko. His expression, however, was serious.

'My apologies,' he said. 'There is a protest going on outside the Vela Ada courthouse.'

Marko briefly kissed Jas before he took the seat across from her, the simple action still making her shiver.

It took her a moment—just a moment—to recall what he'd just said. 'Anything I need to know about?'

Anything that could increase Marko's threat level needed to be considered by her team.

He nodded. 'Senator Božić is being sentenced today. Unfortunately his supporters aren't letting go of their conspiracy theory, or their resolute belief in his innocence.'

Jas was familiar with the situation, of course. The senator's corruption had been discovered twelve months ago, shocking the people of Vela Ada and having far-reaching impacts. Dozens of contracts had been cancelled as the corrupt behaviour had been investigated, with Božić taking bribes to influence tender decisions for several capital work projects.

Businesses had collapsed amidst the scandal—with thousands of innocent workers also losing their jobs.

It was a very messy situation, and one where King Lukas had taken a far more visible role than was usual for the head of state of Vela Ada's constitutional monarchy—given Lukas reigned over Vela Ada, but he did not rule it. That was the role of the elected government.

But the situation had required a sense of unity

despite a fractured parliament, and so Lukas had done his best to hold his country together.

It was primarily why Prince Marko had been needed in Lukas's absence. In times of turmoil, there was something satisfyingly reassuring in the stability of Vela Ada's royal family.

'Lukas—and I—have faith that the investigation was fair and the outcome was correct, and to be honest I'd thought that the protests were over now that the government is helping the innocents caught up in all this...'

Jas had read about how employees of the businesses involved had received one-off payments to go some way towards off setting their financial losses. But not all, of course.

'But it seems not,' he added, then rubbed his forehead in a gesture that had now become familiar to Jas. He did it in contemplation, and also frustration, she'd discovered.

'So there'll be a briefing with Palace Security and the police?'

Marko nodded.

'I don't imagine this will increase my threat level—the issue that these people have is not with me, or even with Lukas.'

He was probably correct. 'When is it?'

'During the opera tonight,' Marko said.

'Of course it is,' Jas said, frustrated. 'But I'll still need to go to the briefing. I'm not delegating this. I'll just meet you at the opera later.'

It wasn't even a question.

Marko smiled, and looked utterly unsurprised. 'I've already organised a car for you.'

Jas arrived at the royal box about ten minutes before intermission.

Even in the muted light, she was stunning in her navy-blue floor-length gown, and with her hair swept up and off her face. She wore jewellery borrowed from the royal collection, so sapphires and diamonds glittered at her ears and décolletage.

Marko stood to greet her, intensely aware that the whole theatre was no longer paying attention to the performance of *La Bohème*—but was instead focused on Jasmine's arrival.

A vague reason had been provided by the palace for Jas's tardiness, although it was possible some members of the public might have guessed at the real reason, given the events of the day. It didn't really matter. There was, of course, intense interest in Jas's career and how she might—or might not—continue to run her business once she was a princess.

But, given that wouldn't actually happen, there'd

been no need for Marko or Jas to provide anything but the barest of answers when asked about it.

Although, if Jas had *actually* been his fiancée, Marko definitely knew the answer.

There was no way she was giving up her career.

He remembered her adamant expression as she'd told him so clearly that she wouldn't be delegating tonight's briefing. Nope. She would *not* have walked away from a career she so obviously loved.

He smiled now as Jas reached his side. He took her hand, and, as always, laced his fingers with hers.

He kissed her—he was definitely taking advantage of this waiver of the no-kissing policy—and then whispered in her ear: 'How did it go?'

'No official change to the threat level, as there's been no credible threat to you, or Lukas. But I'm going to bring in a couple of extras from my team, anyway—I should've done it earlier, really.'

'Why?' Marko said as they settled back into their seats. 'You, and your team, have done an exceptional job.'

'Thank you,' Jas said. 'But I can't possibly be as focused on my protection role while acting as your fiancée. Especially now.'

Below them, the orchestra and soprano were reaching a crescendo, and Marko sensed—thankfully—that the eyes of the theatre were no longer on them.

'Especially now?' Marko asked. He still held her hand loosely, and now drew little squiggles on the delicate skin of her wrist with his thumb.

Jas bumped her shoulder against his, and he could see her smile even as she concentrated on the performance below. 'Don't pretend you don't know exactly how distracting you are.'

And—just because he could—Marko then told Jas—very quietly—all the distracting things he would like to do to her, right now.

If they weren't at the opera, with two bodyguards standing just metres away.

Then later, back at the palace, they did all those distracting things, together.

The next week was…fun.

Fun didn't seem quite the right word, given Jas was, technically, working, but it was definitely accurate.

When she was with Marko, she always seemed to be smiling.

Whether he was teasing her into a laugh, or guiding her through a crowd with the lightest touch at her waist, or patiently translating conversations into English for her—around Marko, she just smiled.

They'd fallen easily into a new normal pattern of behaviour post the 'no kissing' clause. Both wary of any sudden change notifying keen royal watchers of something being up, they were careful not to become dramatically more affectionate in public.

But then, Jas thought Marko was seriously unlikely to *ever* be particularly affectionate in public.

Jas knew that Marko never forgot the scrutiny they were under.

With no further protests following the incarceration of the corrupt senator, and no further intel received from the police, Jas and her team—now expanded by two—simply continued their routine of royal engagements.

This week they had another school visit—this time a secondary school—then a charity auction, and finally, on the weekend, they visited a winery that through its innovative viticulture and harvesting techniques—so Marko told her—was putting the wines of Vela Ada on the international stage.

It was another warm day, and Jas's heels sank slightly into the rich soil as she walked beside Marko between rows upon rows of grape vines. Just ahead of them, the winery owner was their tour guide, and a small group of palace-approved photographers, plus Marko's bodyguards, followed behind.

Their guide didn't speak English, but Jas was taking the opportunity to just enjoy her surroundings. For almost four weeks now she'd spent all her time either at royal engagements, running her company or—for the last week—alone with Marko.

It had all been a blur, really—and stressful at times, too.

As she'd told Marko right from the beginning, she was no actress. And so acting in her fake-fiancée role had been far from easy for her. Even though she'd been playing a variation of herself, any question put to her about their relationship was an opportunity for her to accidentally expose Marko's deception, and she'd felt the weight of that responsibility heavily on her shoulders.

Plus, she was also responsible for Marko's *actual* safety. So there was that, too.

It was probably ridiculous that she felt more comfortable theoretically saving Marko's life than mingling with the Vela Ada hoi polloi—but it was the truth.

Although, now, she definitely did feel herself relaxing into the role. She and Marko knew their back story inside out, and her lies flowed far more easily. She'd also got a lot better at smiling for the cameras—and also *much* better at not looking herself up on the Internet. Nothing was gained from viewing the hundreds of photos taken every time she was out in public with Marko, and definitely not from reading any of the comments. Unsurprisingly, a lot of people weren't super happy such an eligible bachelor was no longer—apparently—available, and she'd stumbled across some not-so-nice remarks.

A brisk breeze whipped its way across the valley, ruffling the loose curls that her stylist had arranged her hair into this morning. Jas smoothed her hair back behind her ears as she looked out across the vines and the undulating hills, and breathed in the scent of damp soil and clean, crisp air.

She might be more relaxed in her role, but it still didn't feel any less crazy. If she stopped for a moment—like now—it just seemed even more fantastical. Right now she could hear the click of a photographer behind her, and of course she knew exactly where her team had positioned themselves to protect Marko—but they were also protecting her.

Marko and the guide had stopped, just ahead. Marko was watching as he waited for her to catch up, his gaze sliding down the shape of her polka-dot sundress before returning to her face with an appreciative smile.

He held out his hand for her as she approached, and then leant forward to press a kiss to her cheek.

As his lips pressed against her skin—just for that moment—Jas allowed herself to indulge in the fantasy that her life had become:

A princess with bodyguards, a hair stylist *and* a make-up artist, a bottomless closet of designer clothing and a constant schedule of glamorous events to attend...

And her very own prince.

Sort of.

Just for a short while.

CHAPTER ELEVEN

JAS WOKE UP before Marko.

He slept flat on his back, she'd discovered. With one arm hooked above his head, and the other hand either across his chest or—just the one time—flung out and laid over hers.

Almost as if he wanted to hold her hand as she slept.

Ha! Jas rolled her eyes as she studied him. Right. She was not one given to overly romantic notions, especially now.

She sat perched on the edge of the bed as she watched his chest rise and fall. She was dressed in T-shirt and jeans, her feet bare and her hair still wet from a shower.

She would much rather stay in bed with Marko. They'd had a late night following a formal dinner with visiting French diplomats and also—she really liked lying in bed with him. And just looking at him—even now, after ten mornings of waking up beside Marko, the novelty had not worn off.

Ten mornings?

Jas mentally recounted before confirming to her-self that—yes—it had definitely been ten morn-ings since she'd last woken up in her own bed. At the moment, the adjacent suite was used more as a closet than a bedroom, and each evening it lit-erally hadn't even occurred to her to return to her own room.

Should it?

Her phone vibrated briefly on the bedside table, signalling she'd received a new email, and the sound was a welcome distraction.

She had a conference call to attend with her team in Hong Kong, but she still had a few minutes before she needed to leave. So she picked up her phone and settled back against the velvet bedhead for a few minutes of email-checking and mindless internet checking.

But the moment she saw the new email her stom-ach plummeted.

The email wasn't signed, and the address was one of those free ones, with a meaningless jumble of letters before the '@'.

But its intent was clear. Jas didn't need to open the attachments to know exactly what they con-tained.

And know exactly what this faceless person

would do with them if she didn't do what he or she wanted.

'Jas?'

Marko had woken, and he'd propped himself up on one elbow.

But for once all those acres of gorgeous olive-toned skin were no distraction. Jas's brain simply raced around in every direction, desperately trying to form a coherent thought, let alone a coherent action.

What was she going to do?

'*Jas,*' Marko said, more firmly now. 'What's going on?'

He sat up, and she could see concern in his gaze.

It was *really* tempting to just blurt it out—to tell him about the email, and the piece of her past that it represented. To share her panic with him and have him help her work out what on earth her next steps might be.

She almost did—she could feel the words, all ready to go, right on the tip of her tongue: *A few years ago I dated a guy I thought was perfect, but...*

But to reveal something so personal, so embarrassing, so painful...

To dump all this on Marko...

Why would she do that? He wasn't her partner; he wasn't her boyfriend.

Their relationship, such as it was, was not based on anything beyond laughter, sex and their fake engagement. Since that afternoon at the beach they had not shared anything personal with each other.

It had been about fun, and mutual attraction.

And that was the way it needed to stay.

If anything, this email simply underlined that. She did *not* want to ever confuse sex for something it wasn't, ever, ever again.

She remembered how her mum had asked if she'd told Marko about her past, and she'd lied so easily.

Well—here she was. It was actually happening. It was the stuff of her nightmares, and Marko *would* need to be told now, but he didn't need to know right this instant. And he definitely didn't need all the messy, emotional details.

On the phone to her mum that day, she'd told herself how he'd react if she did—how he'd judge her. Back then, she'd wavered—but based on what? Why on earth would Marko be different from everyone else?

She looked at him now, and it was so tempting to tell herself that he *would* be different. That if she told him now she wouldn't be left awash with shame and regret.

But that was as silly a romantic notion as Marko holding her hand as she slept.

'Nothing's going on,' she said brightly. Then smiled.

It was a fake smile, though. The first fake smile between them.

Did Marko realise that?

For a moment, she thought he wasn't going to let her get away with it.

But then, maybe he came to the same conclusion Jas had.

Their relationship wasn't about intimacy beyond the physical, and it certainly wasn't about sharing secrets.

'Okay,' he said. 'Good.' He sat up, and swung his legs onto the floor. 'I'm going to go get some breakfast.'

Jas nodded. 'Enjoy!' she said, with that same false breeziness.

Then she got out of bed, put on her sandals, and left Marko's room.

After breakfast Marko went for a run.

Quite a long run, and with his security detail shadowing him, so it was no surprise that by the end of it he was being tailed by a news station van and a paparazzo on a bicycle.

But honestly, today, he didn't really care.

Maybe this was how Lukas dealt with all the attention and intrusion—by just immersing himself within it, rather than fighting it?

If someone really wanted to buy a magazine, or visit a website, that had a photo of him drenched in sweat and breathing heavily, then let them. He didn't care.

Marko's lips quirked upwards. He knew that tomorrow he would definitely care again, just today he couldn't be bothered.

Last night, just before dinner, Lukas had called.

They'd been speaking regularly, but for the first time Lukas had sounded different. Tired.

Really tired.

And he'd told Marko about the ulcers in his mouth, and how they were actually worse than the hours of being hooked up to the cocktail of chemicals that would—Marko desperately hoped—save Lukas's life. He'd joked about his hair loss too, about how for the first time he was the one moulting all over the bathroom, rather than Petra with her mane of golden blonde hair.

Lukas had been deliberately upbeat, and so had Marko.

And it wasn't as if Lukas's fatigue were a surprise. Cancer treatment was exhausting, and Lukas being tired didn't necessarily mean that anything was wrong.

None of what Lukas was experiencing indicated that anything was going wrong.

But still, Marko worried.

Back at the palace, Marko had a shower.

As he grabbed the soap out of the niche in the wall that held his toiletries, he knocked over Jas's little bottle of face scrub. As he righted it he remembered Jas's expression from earlier, as she'd stared, white as a ghost, at her phone.

Something had been wrong; it had been obvious in every tense line of her body, and in her parody of a smile.

But she hadn't wanted to talk to him about it.

Just as he'd decided not to talk to Jas about his concerns for Lukas last night.

Last night he'd told himself that he could handle it. What value was there in confiding in Jas? Of confiding in anyone? He'd managed well enough this far into his adult life without doing so.

Except for that day at the beach—but then, he had no plans to repeat that.

So he could hardly challenge Jas for doing the same—for handling things on her own.

And if there was anyone who could handle anything life threw at her, it was Jasmine Gallagher.

He raised his face into the firm spray of water, squeezing his eyes shut as water sluiced over his body.

But, even as he instinctively knew that she probably wouldn't want or appreciate his concern, he couldn't just switch it off.

He got out of the shower, towelled himself dry, and made a decision.

He didn't need to know the details—but he needed to go find her.

Right now. And make sure she was okay.

After her conference call with her team, Jas organised for Ivan to come meet her in the small *salon*—as the palace staff referred to the small reception room where Jas had been working over the past few weeks—to discuss the email.

She sat on a brocade single armchair with spindly legs, the small coffee table before her holding her now-closed laptop, her printer and a small mountain of printed plans, maps and schedules.

Her makeshift office was quite incongruent

with the room full of antique furniture and the oil paintings of—Jas assumed—Pavlovic ancestors, all with identical severe expressions.

Ivan sat across from her, in a matching armchair, and listened as she explained her situation, and her suggestions as to what they should do next.

Fortunately, Ivan agreed with her approach, but there were others within the palace that would need to be consulted—there were protocols and procedures to be followed and expert advice to be canvassed.

But first, they needed to tell Marko.

As if reading their minds Marko materialised at the doorway.

'Jas,' he said. 'I was—'

But then his gaze drifted to Ivan, and he went silent.

Ivan stood, immediately. 'I'll leave you to discuss this with His Highness,' he said.

'No,' Jas said, more sharply then she'd intended. 'I think it's best that you stay.'

Ivan barely raised his eyebrows as he resettled in his chair. He was good at his job, Jas had to give him that. The epitome of discretion.

She stood, straightened her shoulders, and said to Marko: 'Please, take a seat.'

She was being deliberately formal. They had a

situation to deal with, so it made sense to be so, she'd decided.

Marko just nodded. She'd become used to him kissing her, or at least touching her, whenever they were in close proximity.

He did neither now. She didn't *want* him to, right now, of course. But still, she definitely noticed that he didn't.

Marko took a seat on the two-seater armchair between Ivan and Jas, but he turned his body to face her, and not the valet.

'Jas,' he said firmly as she took her own seat. 'Are you okay?'

She nodded, equally firmly. 'Of course. We have a situation I need to brief you about.'

His expression was unreadable. 'Okay.'

Jas took a deep breath.

'This morning I received an email from an anonymous sender who is trying to blackmail me,' she began, ensuring her tone was matter-of-fact. 'He has some photos of me.' She swallowed. 'Uh, naked photos of me, that he will release to the press if I don't meet his demands. Which are basically for me to pay him a lot of money.'

Marko simply nodded.

Jas desperately searched his gaze for his reaction, for the glint of *something*.

Shock. Disappointment. Disgust.

But she saw nothing.

'Fortunately the photos are relatively tasteful. I took them myself, actually, selfies…' She swallowed again. 'Anyway. While I definitely wouldn't have chosen for the photos to be seen by anybody, and I'd actually hoped to never see them again—Ivan and I agreed that the best thing to do is to defuse the situation by issuing a press release about their existence. If I'm lucky, this person will then just disappear. Or maybe he'll publish the photos, or sell them—I don't know. But at least we get to start the narrative, rather than respond to it.'

'Ensure any media organisation who publishes the photos is blacklisted by the palace,' Marko said in a clipped, authoritative tone. He still held her gaze, but Jas could still read nothing in it.

'Of course,' Ivan said.

'Plus explore any legal options we have.'

For the next few minutes, Ivan discussed next steps with them both, but Jas barely participated.

What was Marko thinking?

Right now, needing to know what Marko thought was killing her—more than the photos, more than anything.

Ivan stood up and exited the room.

Marko's gaze had barely moved from hers, either. It was excruciating.

But then, the moment Ivan left them alone, something in his eyes shifted.

Jas squeezed her own eyes shut, and let out a long, slow breath as her stupid, naïve bubble of hope that Marko would be different painfully deflated.

'You must think I'm such an idiot,' she said, eyes still closed. 'Naïve, right? Stupid? Thoughtless?'

All the words she'd heard before echoed in her brain.

'I should've thought to tell you earlier, but I was so sure the photos had been deleted. And that my ex would never—' She stopped. No. Marko didn't care about the details. He was just like the rest of them. Was it too much to ask that just *one* person wouldn't blame her?

No, not just one person. *Marko.*

She'd *so badly* wanted him to be different. The realisation that he wasn't shocked her as much as the arrival of that awful email.

'I'm sorry—' she began.

'Jas,' he said firmly. 'Stop. You have nothing to apologise for.'

Jas shook her head, eyes still closed.

She was being ridiculous, even within this ridiculous situation. But she couldn't bear to see the judgment in his eyes.

He was saying the right thing, but he didn't really mean it.

'Look at me,' he said, louder now. Demanding. Then more softly. 'Jas, please.'

Finally, she did.

It was still there, in his gaze. What she'd seen.

But now—now that she took more than a moment to acknowledge it, to interpret it—she realised what she was really seeing.

The look in his eyes matched his body language—the tension in his shoulders, the bulging of his biceps, the way his hands had formed into fists.

He was angry. Furious.

But not with her.

Definitely not with her.

'You have nothing to apologise for,' Marko repeated. 'You're not the one threatening to circulate stolen photographs.' That he thought the person doing so should be *very* sorry was obvious in his poisonous tone. '*You* haven't done anything wrong.'

Jas sagged a little in her seat, disbelieving.

'Jasmine,' Marko said firmly. 'You aren't stupid, or naïve, or thoughtless. I would *never* think that.' Then he shrugged. 'Besides, why wouldn't you take naked photos of yourself?' He grinned now. 'You're hot.'

The comment was so unexpected amidst all the tension that Jas burst out laughing.

But now he was more serious again. 'I know all about how it feels to have your privacy invaded, Jas. I'm so sorry you're going through this.'

His words were sincere, and for a moment Jas was tempted to say more. To let him know there was more to the story. To trust this man who hadn't judged her, who wasn't angry with her—who hadn't blamed her for any of this.

But instead, she said: 'But I don't think anyone's got a photo of you *naked*, Marko.'

'True,' he said. 'Want to take some?'

This time, they laughed together.

They didn't take any naked photographs.

Instead, Marko left Jas in the salon to continue working, while he filled his day working with Ivan and the palace protocol staff to determine the best way to protect Jasmine from the *vrag*—the devil— who was blackmailing her. Privately, he imagined exactly what he would do if he ever met the guy, and it definitely involved him *never* being able to hurt Jas again.

Although, it wasn't as if Jas needed him.

She'd worked out her plan of attack without him, and had included him in the discussion as a stakeholder she was bringing up to speed. *Not* as her... *what*, exactly?

Guy she was sleeping with? He *was* that.

Boyfriend? No.

But surely that lack shouldn't move him behind *Ivan* in the chain of communication?

It appeared it did.

Maybe that shouldn't sit so uncomfortably with him, but it did. Who would've thought—Marko Pavlovic was disappointed that a woman *hadn't* told him something obviously private and emotional?

Actually, he realised, it wasn't disappointment he was feeling.

He was hurt.

Which was stupid, and selfish, as what Jas was going through was definitely *not* about him. And he knew that Jas had gone to Ivan based on the premise of their relationship: casual, fun. No deeply personal secret revelations.

But still, he wished she'd come to him, first.

Did that mean he wanted *more* than fun with Jas?

He hadn't worked that out by the time he went down to meet her for dinner, once again out on the terrace. He didn't really even know what it would mean if he did.

But as it turned out, he didn't need to work out anything—or maybe it had been worked out for him—because shortly after he sat down at their table, a member of staff passed on a message from Jasmine:

'Ms Gallagher sends her apologies. She's having an early night tonight.'

After dinner, Marko was unsurprised to discover Jas had not spent her early night in his room— which had been effectively hers for a week and a half—but in her own.

So into his own bed Marko collapsed, alone.

Jas did not have a good night's sleep.

She was most of the way through a very strong coffee when Marko strode out onto the terrace the following morning.

She hadn't been sure whether she'd even see him

today. They had nothing scheduled, so there was no requirement for them to do so. And after yesterday—and especially after last night—would he even want to?

Would he have seen her decision to spend the night alone as a snub?

Or would he not even care? Would he have been thrilled to have some time to himself?

Last night she'd told herself that he *wouldn't* care. He might be a bit annoyed she hadn't told him personally that she was sleeping in her own bed, but seriously—ten nights in a row sharing a room was surely enough. They needed a break from each other.

But, as she saw him now, with dark smudges under his eyes that she couldn't read at all, she wasn't so sure.

Even so, she did exactly what she'd planned.

She stood up, and met him as he approached.

She rose on tiptoes, and pressed her lips to his cheek in greeting.

She *didn't* want what they had to end, not yet. But last night…

Last night it had scared her how much she'd wanted to tell Marko everything. To cry in his arms—rather than alone in her room—at the embarrassment and overwhelming sense of hurt and anger she felt deep within her bones. How *dared* Stuart—or one of the men with whom he'd shared her photos, or even, although it was a slim chance, whoever had hacked into his account—do this to her?

But would Marko want to just hold her while she cried?

She didn't know. It wasn't fair to expect he would. And so she had slept—a little—alone.

'Did you have a good night's sleep without me hogging the covers?' she said brightly as she stepped back. His unshaved jaw had been rough against her lips.

But Marko didn't answer her.

Instead, he stepped forward, and dragged her into his arms.

And, without a word, he kissed her. Kissed her thoroughly, until her eyes slid shut and her arms wrapped behind his neck, desperately pulling herself closer.

Kissed her until her knees felt useless, and she wished the hands bunched in the fabric of her singlet could whip it over her head, and she could push his own T-shirt up so she could press even closer against him, skin to skin.

Kissed her until she had no idea about anything

but how his lips and tongue felt against hers, and how hard and strong his body felt pressed against her own.

Then, he stepped back.

They were both breathing heavily, and now she could certainly read Marko's gaze—there was no doubt she was seeing a mirror of the want and need in hers.

But then, suddenly, all of that was gone.

His expression was once again indecipherable.

It was so abrupt, Jas would've hardly believed he'd just been kissing her if she couldn't still taste him on her lips, and feel the abrasion of his stubble on her skin.

'I'm visiting Lukas today,' he said. 'They'll expect you to come with me.'

Not—*I would like you to come with me.* And not even a question as to whether she'd like to go.

Marko expected her to accompany him out to the Pavlovic Estate today to visit his brother and his wife.

But he didn't actually want her to come. He just needed her to, because they were supposed to be engaged.

'Okay,' she said. 'No problem. I'll go get changed.'

It was her job, after all. She shouldn't feel weird

about it—that Marko didn't really want her by his side as he visited his unwell brother.

It made sense. This was definitely beyond the boundaries of their fun, short-term relationship. Just as yesterday's photo saga had been, too.

Boundaries were good. *She* was the one who'd been so sure to strengthen them last night.

Maybe it was just the contrast—to share a kiss that felt so intense, and so intimate…and now to feel a million miles apart?

Yes, Jas decided. It was.

It had to be.

CHAPTER TWELVE

GIVEN THEIR ENTIRE relationship had evolved from a fake relationship, Marko wondered if maybe it was to be expected that interactions between himself and Jas could sometimes feel false.

But the thing was, they hadn't until now.

Even right at the beginning, when they'd barely known each other.

Even then, Jas had always been genuine. She'd always been herself.

It was why he'd kissed her before, out on the terrace.

When she'd asked how he'd slept—and he'd *known* it was a line she'd prepared as he'd recognised the subtly different tone she'd used with reporters when reciting the story of how they'd supposedly met—he'd *hated* that she was pretending for him.

And so he'd kissed her. To see, maybe, if the spark—no, the fireworks—between them was fake, too.

But it wasn't. That connection between them, the physical one, anyway, burned even brighter, if anything. For long moments after he'd finally stepped away from her he'd had no idea what his plans for the day had been, beyond kissing Jas a hell of a lot more.

Then he'd remembered.

So, here they were.

In just a single car today, with security based at the estate where his mother lived full time after retiring from public life after his father's death, and where his brother would be living for the duration of his treatment.

The car entered between tall stone pillars and a wrought-iron gate, then weaved its way down a long, winding driveway to reach the house.

Compared to the palace, it was a very modest building, just two storeys tall and built out of stone and a red-tiled roof like nearly every other house across Vela Ada. It had sprawled from the original centuries-old building with a succession of additions by previous generations, and at the rear a white-painted pergola stretched across much of its length, covered in lush, twining grape vines.

As their car came to a stop Petra and his mother raced from the front door to greet them.

Behind them, moving much more slowly, was Lukas.

But to even see him outside, the sun glinting off his brother's dark hair, did much to release the vice-like pressure on Marko's chest.

Just as he went to exit the car Jas grabbed his hand.

He went still. They hadn't touched, or spoken, since they'd left the palace.

'I won't get in your way,' Jas said, meeting Marko's gaze. 'I promise.'

There was lots more in her hazel eyes: concern—for him?—an attempt at reassurance, understanding…

'I know,' he said. He'd never doubted she'd understand what he needed today. 'Thank you,' he added.

And as he said it he realised his thank you wasn't only because of what she'd said, but also simply because she was here with him.

Then he got out of the car, and strode over to his family, before he could consider for a moment what that might mean.

Petra took Jas for a tour of the surrounding landscape while Marko caught up with Lukas.

They walked through an olive grove that

stretched in rows from the rear of the grand old home, and then past a small orchard to a large vegetable plot. Clumps of lavender and rosemary scented the air, and the sun ducked in and out from behind powder-puff clouds.

Petra did most of the talking as she described the history of the property and the Pavlovic family—but when they arrived at the vegetables, she clapped her hands together in excitement.

'Now *this*,' she said, 'is the only good thing to come out of Lukas's illness—I finally have time to garden.'

Jas noticed the freshly sown rows of dirt, and the carefully handwritten signs stuck into the ground before each one. Then there were the established rows—of beans and tomatoes winding their way up stick pyramids, and other neat lines of green fronds that Jas couldn't identify. Their signs were of no help: *krumpir, mrkve…*

'You grew all this?' Jas asked, surprised.

She couldn't imagine Petra working in a garden—even now in casual jeans, blouse and sandals she was just *so* elegant. But as Jas watched the Queen absently yanked some recalcitrant weeds from the rich, dark brown earth.

'Yes,' she said, beaming. 'I come from a family of market gardeners. Growing up, I was in charge of at least one crop for the weekly *tržnica*—a market—and I've never really lost interest in growing my own vegetables. I just don't get much of a chance nowadays, although I do help the chef with her herb garden at the palace.'

'You met Lukas at university, right?' Jas asked, trying to connect the dots as to how the daughter of market gardeners became a queen.

Petra smiled. 'Yes. In Split. A long way from my family's market garden in Korcula,' she said, reading Jas's mind. 'My father was very old-fashioned, and he was so worried that tertiary education would make me leave Korcula Island for ever. And as it turns out, he was right.'

'Do you ever miss it?' asked Jas.

Petra shrugged. 'Sometimes. Not so much Korcula—or even Croatia—but my family, definitely. And also the simplicity of that life.' She paused, then smiled. 'Why? Are you missing Australia?'

'A bit,' Jas said honestly. 'It's been so crazy these last few weeks, I almost crave my normal life in Canberra.'

'*Almost* crave,' Petra said, her gaze knowing. 'I'd bet Marko is pretty good at distracting you from your homesickness.'

Jas gave a shocked laugh.

Petra shrugged. 'I'm married to his brother, remember,' she said. Then winked, before heading down along a row of lettuce, pausing occasionally to pull up more rogue weeds.

Jas hurried along behind her.

'It's great to see Marko so happy with you,' Petra said, over her shoulder. 'My mother-in-law is *very* proud of Marko for stepping in for Lukas, so I've seen heaps of the photos and footage of you together.'

Jas didn't really know how to respond to this. The *Queen* and the *Dowager Queen* of Vela Ada had been looking at photos of *her*?

Well, of Prince Marko mostly, she was sure.

But her, too.

Another thing to add to her list of things she'd never thought would happen to her.

Along with contributing to the fact the photos making an elderly woman happy were based on a lie.

Although…if she was honest, they *had* been having fun together at the many, many events they'd been attending. So the smiles Petra and the Dowager Queen had seen had been real, at least.

Petra had stopped and was looking at Jas as if waiting for her to say something.

'Um—' Jas said. 'Aren't engaged people supposed to look happy together?'

'I'd hope so,' Petra said, 'but Marko...' She paused. 'I haven't seen him like this since before his dad passed away. Even today—I know he's worried about Lukas, but there is just something *different* about him.'

'He's taking his role seriously,' Jas said. 'He knows he needs to get better at engaging with the public, and with the media, even though it doesn't sit comfortably with him. He's working really hard.'

Too late, Jas realised how defensive she sounded. As if she was trying to convince Petra that Marko *wasn't* actually happy.

Petra just studied her curiously, and then turned and walked off again—this time a few rows over. She dropped to a squat to pick a handful of plump red strawberries from amongst clusters of deep green leaves, and then stood and gave half of her harvest to Jas.

'Lukas is complicated,' Petra said. 'I know Marko is complicated too. I've known him nearly fifteen years, and I don't *really* know him. Not really. So, maybe I don't actually know if he's happy or not.'

Jas shook her head.

What had she done?

How had such a simple conversation gone so wrong?

It would've been so easy to just smile, and laugh, and say something about how happy she and Marko were. That was what Petra had expected her to say. It was what *anyone* would say.

It was what she'd said when responding to a hundred similar observations over the past few weeks. She'd even got creative and embellished: they'd been *blissfully* happy, and *incredibly* happy and *happier than I thought was possible!*

But as it had been that very first night, when she'd first met Petra, there was something about the Queen that made Jas find it near impossible to lie. Or not even lie—but to speak for Marko.

Because, what did she know about how happy Marko was? Who was she to speak for him? Beyond their physical relationship, she knew nothing about what he was thinking or feeling. He'd said not a word about Lukas's illness to her since that day at the beach. He'd confided nothing in her, about anything. Sure, he smiled a lot around her, but was he truly *happy*?

So she racked her brain for something to say… *anything* to say that would stop Petra looking at her so seriously. Preferably something that was also true.

'Marko makes *me* happy,' she said.

The words came out in a rush in the end, before Jas could stop them.

Petra's gaze was wise and assessing. 'Good,' she said simply. 'Now, try the strawberries.'

Lunch had been fine.

He, Lukas and their mother had been settled in their chairs beneath the canopy of grape vines, a literal feast spread out before them upon a blue-checked tablecloth, when Jas and Petra had returned from their walk.

Jas had come straight over to kiss him, briefly, on the cheek. In that instant he'd inhaled the scent of sun and the sunscreen on her shoulders, plus her familiar citrus and spice perfume.

But she hadn't lingered; instead she'd taken her seat across from him and barely touched him again until they'd left. She'd charmed his mother over lunch and laughed at all of Lukas's terrible jokes—but with him she'd still been as distant as she'd been all morning. Maybe even more so, actually.

But not in a way that anyone else would notice, although Marko certainly had.

In the car on the way home she'd asked him about Lukas, but Marko had been pretty matter-of-fact: he was doing as well as could be expected. Prognosis was still good.

After that it had just been silence.

Silence until now, as they stood, alone, together, in the hallway outside both of their rooms.

It was late afternoon.

Marko had vaguely considered going for a run. Or going down to the gym in the palace basement.

He didn't know what Jas planned to do with the rest of her day. Work, probably.

'Jas—' Marko said, and then stopped.

He'd meant to say he'd see her that evening for dinner, but found he couldn't.

'Jas,' he started, again. She just stood there, looking at him, her hands loosely knotted in front of her. She looked beautiful, even with her hair in a simple ponytail and without the efforts of her make-up artist. His gaze was locked with hers, and in hers he saw…uncertainty? Or was he just projecting how he suddenly felt? 'I—'

But Jas halted his words when she stepped close, curled her fingers into his hair, and pulled his mouth down to hers. Hard.

It was a determined kiss, almost an *angry* kiss, and definitely a frustrated kiss.

Marko kissed her back with all of his own frustration of the past twenty-four hours, and of the way things with Jas now didn't feel easy. He kissed her with frustration that she wasn't bumping her shoulder against his when they walked, or asking him to teach her Slavic swear words in the car. Her eyes weren't sparkling when she looked at him, and her lips weren't quirking at even the silliest little joke he'd make.

He didn't fully understand what had happened, but he knew he didn't like this new distance between them. Right now, the best way to remedy that seemed to be to get as close as it was possible for two people to be.

Thankfully, as Jas yanked his shirt upwards and popped open his buttons, she certainly seemed to be thinking the exact same thing.

His own hands tugged the elastic from her hair and then slid beneath her silk blouse to caress hot, perfect skin, and press her as close against him as possible. His hardness against her softness, her breasts squashed against the bare chest her impatient fingers had now revealed.

He somehow backed her against the door to her room, and part of him was lucid enough to reach for the door handle—before he was completely distracted by the way Jas was shifting her hips against his.

Then all he could focus on was lifting her up so

she could wrap her jeans-clad legs around his waist, and kissing her harder: hot, and long, and raw.

At some point, as he kissed Jas's jaw and neck and made his way downwards, she suddenly whispered in his ear: 'I think we have company.'

He followed her gaze to an obviously hastily abandoned bucket and mop, lying haphazardly down the hall.

He grinned as he finally opened the door to Jas's suite.

'I'll apologise to the staff later,' he murmured.

He could feel Jas smile against his cheek as he carried her into the room. 'They'll understand,' she said. 'Everyone thinks we're madly in love.'

Marko took a moment to laugh in response, her blithe comment oddly jarring. But he didn't have time to think about it, in fact, now that he'd deposited Jas onto her bed, and she was looking up at him, her shirt and bra askew, and her eyes hot and seductive…

Right now was definitely not the time for thinking.

Right now was all about how Jas made him feel.

Jas closed her eyes as she let the warm water pour over her, the shower pressure just high enough to provide a satisfying sting against her scalp.

When she opened her eyes, Marko—also in her shower with her—smiled.

He reached out, running a finger beneath her left eye. 'I hadn't realised you were wearing make-up,' he said.

'Are you nicely saying I have panda eyes?' she asked as she reached around him for her face wash—before remembering it was still in Marko's bathroom.

The realisation was irrationally annoying—after all, she'd first realised she was face-wash-less this morning, and she'd managed well enough then.

But now, with Marko here…

Should she bring her face wash back? Or leave it where it was as now she'd go back to staying in Marko's room? Or should she buy another one, so that she and Marko could continue to be all free and casual and non-committal about whatever they had going on?

Marko's finger now traced the smudge beneath her other eye, and then, so gently, traced the shape of her cheekbones, jaw, and then lips. His touch—so sensual, and so delicate, in delicious contrast to the water still firm against her back—made her eyes slide shut.

'What are you thinking about?' he asked, low and soft.

'Toiletries,' she muttered.

'Pardon me?'

Jas's eyes snapped open. Marko looked at her curiously.

He stood very close to her. They'd showered together before, but Jas hadn't tired of looking at Marko soaking wet. He was almost beautiful rather than simply handsome, with water droplets caught in his eyelashes, and the hard, wet edges and planes of his shoulders, chest and abdominal muscles.

'Jas?' he asked.

'I want to know where to put my face wash,' she said honestly.

'Okay,' he said, his brow creasing. 'Is this a metaphor for something?'

She nodded. 'Yes. I don't like not knowing what's really going on here. It's been weird between us since yesterday—and I don't like it.'

'Neither do I,' Marko said bluntly.

He was looking at her intensely, but Jas couldn't interpret it.

'What do you want?' he asked.

Ah—Jas could understand it now. It was subtle, but there. The tension in his shoulders, and in his jaw. Just as she'd felt when she'd made her joke about them—apparently—being madly in love.

'I wanted to tell you about the photos yesterday,' she said. 'I thought it wasn't appropriate to—I mean, it was pretty serious. Not really part of our fun and no-strings arrangement, right?' Even though she wasn't cold, she rubbed her hands up and down her upper arms. 'But I realised that I don't like having sex with someone that I can't talk to about stuff like that. I mean—I love having sex with you, but—'

She shook her head, trying to refocus.

'Look, for as long as this lasts, I'd like to be able to talk to you. And I want you to talk to me. Otherwise, maybe it's best I just go get my face wash from your bathroom, and we end this now.'

Jas realised, too late, that she could very well be about to be dumped while naked.

But then—of course—she hadn't planned any of this.

'For as long as this lasts,' Marko repeated.

Jas nodded. 'Yes,' she said. 'Whether it's for another week or the rest of my time as your fake fiancée.'

Only now did Marko release the tension in his shoulders.

Oh—he'd thought she was asking for more—something beyond their contracted time together.

Marko makes me happy.

Everyone thinks we're madly in love.

Her own words echoed traitorously inside her head.

No.

This was never about for ever. She didn't *want* for ever. Or rather—she didn't trust it.

Plus, that didn't even matter—Marko *clearly* didn't want for ever, anyway.

But did he still want 'right now'?

Marko still hadn't agreed with her. His gaze travelled across her face, and Jas realised she was holding her breath.

Then—he stepped out of the shower.

He grabbed a fluffy white towel off a hook, and as Jas watched rubbed himself dry, and then wrapped it low around his hips.

Then, he grabbed another towel, stepped back to the shower, and reached behind Jas to turn off the water.

Suddenly, Jas was freezing cold, regardless of the room's perfect climate control.

'Here,' he said, handing her the towel. 'I've been wanting to talk to you about Lukas for days, but I'm not going to talk about my brother and my dad while you're standing in front of me naked in the shower.'

Jas gave a shocked burst of laughter.

Then she took the towel, and said gently, 'You can talk to me any time.'

'I know,' he said with a crooked smile. 'How about we start now?'

CHAPTER THIRTEEN

MARKO HADN'T MADE his decision when he'd got out of that shower, or even as he'd wrapped the towel around his waist.

If Jas had told him about being blackmailed as soon as she'd received the email, he definitely would've listened, and he definitely would've been there to support her—but clearly, she hadn't believed that. And to be honest, she really had no reason to believe he would.

But being prepared to listen to Jas—in fact, *wanting* to be there for Jas—was quite another thing from revealing his own emotions to her.

He hadn't been willing to share anything with anyone for such a long time, he wasn't even sure if he was capable of doing so now.

But in the end, it had been Jas—standing in the shower, as naked and vulnerable as it was possible to be—that had made his decision obvious.

He wasn't walking away from her.

It seemed that right now he needed Jas in a multi-

tude of ways: bodyguard, fiancée, lover and now...
confidante.

But now was not for ever.

And now was what he needed.

They sat, sprawled, on Jas's unmade bed, both
wearing their monogrammed palace bathrobes.
He'd organised for dinner to be brought up to the
room, and they each held glasses of *maraština*
wine.

He just talked.

About Lukas, and what it was like growing up
with him. And then about his father. About how
he'd felt when his father was first diagnosed with
cancer, and how—after he'd got over the initial
shock—he'd been so adamant that his dad would
be okay. Because, of course, his father had had access to the world's best oncologists, the most cut-
ting-edge treatments—Marko had been so sure
that doctors and science would cure him.

Or maybe it had just been his way of dealing
with it all.

His dad actually *had* responded well to his initial treatment. But a year later the cancer had returned, and that original treatment had been less
effective a second time. Other treatments hadn't
worked. And then—initially slowly, but later far
more rapidly—his strong, fit, powerful father had

deteriorated. And eventually, with his mother holding his dad's hand and Lukas and Marko on the other side of the bed, holding onto each other... his father had died.

He'd rushed out of the hospital blindly.

People had been yelling—his brother, his mother, their bodyguards—for him to stop, to wait.

But he couldn't. He'd just needed to move. To not be in that hospital room any longer, sitting across from his horrifically still father.

So he'd raced out of the main entrance—which, of course, had been stupid. What had he expected? If he'd thought it through for even a second he would've known what to expect. He would've known that to run anywhere but out of that door was a better option.

But he hadn't been thinking, he'd been feeling. Feeling emotions he'd barely been aware he'd possessed. Pain and grief and this deep, echoing sense of loss that made him feel sick and empty and impossible. As if this couldn't possibly be happening. His father couldn't possibly be dead.

King Josip's death hadn't been announced yet, so he supposed it wasn't entirely the paparazzi's fault. Because, really, they hadn't known they were photographing a son who had just lost his dad. A man who hadn't even begun to think about con-

cealing his grief. A man who shouldn't have had to conceal anything.

Later he would, though. Over the next days, and weeks, and months he would draw a curtain over how he really felt.

The papers had got their photographs that day. And of course they'd published them, even when they had heard of the King's death. That was definitely the paparazzi's fault. To print those raw photos that exposed everything, exposed emotions he hadn't even been able to let his mother and brother see, and yet they'd been shown to the world...

But he'd learnt, of course. Years later, he was still hiding.

Until now. Until Jasmine.

'I don't want Lukas to die,' Marko said, sinking into the pillows and staring up at the ceiling.

It was such an obvious thing to want, and such an obvious thing to say—and yet he hadn't said it, to anyone, until right at this moment. He'd barely allowed himself to think it.

He heard a clink as Jas rested her glass somewhere, and then the rustling of sheets as she crawled across the bed to where he lay, propped amongst a mountain of pillows.

She met his gaze briefly, and he nodded his permission just before she settled in beside him, curled against his side, her head resting on his chest.

She rested one hand against his chest, and one of his hands found itself in her hair, absently tangling the long strands loosely around his fingers.

'I know he's doing well. I know he's supposed to survive this. But I still worry. I just—'

His voice cracked, and he swallowed.

'I try to be positive for Lukas. I mean, it doesn't help anyone if I'm all doom and gloom. And he seems pretty upbeat too, but then—maybe he's doing the same as me?' Marko shook his head as this occurred to him. 'Maybe all the Pavlovic men are being stoic and non-communicative about how they really feel.'

'I'd say that's a strong possibility,' Jas said, and he could hear the smile in her voice.

Marko talked a bit more, and none of it was anything groundbreaking, or unexpected. He didn't have an epiphany or anything.

But it still helped. Just voicing the fears he'd kept locked in his head seemed to help, even if the fears themselves weren't going anywhere.

After a while Marko fell silent, and he watched as Jas rose and fell against his chest as he breathed. Eventually, Jas shifted, and hauled herself further up his body, so she could kiss him on the mouth.

With her lips still brushing his, she said: 'Thank you for trusting me.'

He kissed her back, because that was it exactly—the reason why he'd been so intensely private for so many years: trust.

First, it was the obvious type of trust. The trust that the person he told was not secretly recording the conversation with plans to sell it to the highest bidder.

Secondly, and—he realised—more importantly, trust that the person he told would not change their opinion of him once he did. *This* was what he'd been unable to find until now.

Maybe it was something to do with the intensity of their current arrangement: the fake fiancée lie they shared, the amount of time they were spending together, the incredible sex…

Whatever it was, he *did* trust Jas to see him for the man he actually was.

And that was…liberating.

He laughed out loud. *Liberating?* Now he *was* having some sort of weird, out-of-body epiphany. And an overreaction. He liked having Jas to talk to—it was no more than that.

'Laughter,' Jas said, her head now back on his chest, 'is not the reaction I'm looking for when

I'm wrapped around a man in nothing more than some terry towelling.'

Immediately Marko rolled Jas onto her back as she shrieked with laughter, so he loomed above her, his hands bracketing her face.

'Is this more like it?' he asked.

But as he watched he saw the playfulness fade from her eyes.

'Want to see some naked photos of me?' she said.

He said no, quite firmly, but Jas persisted.

'I don't need to see them,' he said.

'Odds are you're going to, eventually,' Jas pointed out. The palace's press release was scheduled for the following day.

'No, I won't,' Marko said. 'Anyone who looks at those photos is a—' And he then said a string of Slavic words that—from the few she recognised— Jas was pretty sure were the foulest, filthiest terms possible.

Jas gently pushed against his shoulders, and immediately Marko rolled away. Jas sat up, and then reached for her phone on the bedside table.

'I *want* you to see the photos,' she said. Then, looking up from the screen, she added: 'I think I need you to. Up until now everyone—except the original recipient—who's seen them has done so without my permission. I'd like to make a decision for someone to see them—and that someone is you.'

'Everyone?'

But she'd get to that in a moment. For now, she simply handed the phone to Marko.

He just held it—without looking anywhere near it—for what felt like ages, and so Jas scooted off the bed to the bureau, where their bottle of white wine still nestled in its ice bucket, although it was mostly ice water, now.

She'd left her glass on Marko's bedside table, so she strode over to it, aiming for nonchalance. 'Would you like another?'

He shook his head.

'Just look at the stupid photos,' she said. *'Please.'*

And then, with her back to him, she busied herself with pouring a glass of wine. Reflected in the mirror above the bureau she saw Marko finally scroll through her phone, and as he did she closed her eyes and breathed out. Long and slow.

She took a long, long sip from her glass before she finally turned around to face Marko again.

He'd laid the phone screen-down on her bed.

'You look beautiful in the photos,' he said quietly.

'Thank you,' she said. 'I remember being pretty pleased with them at the time.'

Marko nodded, but didn't say anything more.

She knew this was her cue—after all, she'd just allowed Marko to talk, and now it was her turn.

'Umm—' she began, and then stopped. Swallowed, and straightened her shoulders. 'I had a boyfriend a few years ago,' she said, her tone now strong and clear. 'Stuart. We worked together, actually. He was a sergeant. Not in the same unit as me at the Australian National Police, but we shared the same building, and worked together on some jobs.' She still held her wine glass, but now she just swirled the liquid around a bit, and didn't drink. 'He was a few years older than me. Very handsome, very successful, and very well respected. And very charming. I fell for him, hard. It wasn't like any other relationship I'd had—although, honestly, I haven't had that many.'

If Marko found any of this uncomfortable, he didn't reveal it in any way.

'We'd been together a few months, although we hadn't told anyone at work. Stuart had been really clear on that—and he made it sound like he was protecting *me*. That if things didn't work out between us, that it wouldn't look good if I was the girl who'd had some fling with a guy at work.' She paused now, to let her gaze drift from where it had been focused on her phone, to meet again with

Marko's. 'Obviously that's stupid—why should *I* be the one worried about my reputation, and not him? But that was just the culture really—I worked with eighty-five per cent men. I knew they *would* judge me. Back then, though, that reality didn't make me angry. I just accepted it.'

Briefly, Jas considering moving to sit beside Marko, but she felt as if her bare feet were glued to the plush carpet.

'Anyway, after a few months I guess I sensed that maybe Stuart was drifting away. He cancelled on me a few times. Wasn't always sleeping over. That kind of thing. Although when we were together he still said all the right things—which I now know was more about keeping me on the hook rather than having any basis in truth. But at the time, obviously, I didn't realise that. And I *did* want the spark of the start of our relationship back. So—I decided to send him some sexy photos.'

Jas did take a long drink of her wine now.

'So it was all my idea, not his, if that's what you're wondering. And at the time, it was kind of fun. I mean, it felt pretty risqué, a bit naughty…'

She closed her eyes.

'Actually, even now, I'm not ashamed of the photos. Not at all.'

Her tone was challenging, as if she expected Marko to argue with her.

'You did nothing wrong,' he said, repeating his words from yesterday. 'The photos are beautiful.'

She shook her head, not really wanting to acknowledge a compliment right now. 'My mistake wasn't in taking the photos, but in who I sent them to. And I worked that out *very* quickly. I took the photos on a Saturday night, and Stuart loved them, of course. We spent the day together on Sunday. And then, on Monday, at work, things were different.'

Jas finished her wine, then placed it, with hands that were shaking just a little, onto the tray beside the ice bucket.

'I told myself I was being paranoid. That I was imagining things. But by lunch it was obvious what had happened—there was too much smirking, or suddenly cut-short conversations for it to be anything else. Stuart wasn't responding to my text messages, and he wouldn't answer his phone, so in the end I had to go into his office to confront him. I asked if he'd sent the photos to anyone, and he promised on his mother's life that he hadn't. But—and maybe he did have a shred of humanity, or maybe he realised that I was about to start screaming at him—he did admit to showing them to a couple of the guys.'

She rolled her eyes. *A couple of the guys.* Right. The moment he'd admitted what he'd done had been shocking. Part of her, even then, hadn't wanted to believe it was real. That the man she'd thought she'd loved would do something like this to her.

And aside from that, the gross invasion of her privacy was simply horrific. To think of so many people having looked at her body, judged her body, without her consent…

Even now her stomach churned.

'I watched him delete the photos from his phone, and then I went straight to HR to find out what I could do. I couldn't keep on working in those conditions. Team is everything in the police, and now I felt like I could trust no one. I'm sure some of the guys didn't look at the photos. Many, probably. But who had?

'So I asked if I could make a complaint or something. Do *something*. Have some sort of agency, you know? But the couple of people I spoke to focused more on the fact I'd taken the photos, rather than the fact Stuart shared them with what felt like half the department. They seemed to care more about *my* "poor decisions" than Stuart's. I have no idea if their view reflected the relevant policy or procedure or whatever, but I wasn't about to find out. I've told you before about the frustrations of being a woman in the police force, but most of the time I could deal with it. I could focus on the bigger picture. From that moment, as the worst day of my life suddenly became *my* fault, I'd had enough. So I quit.'

'And started Gallagher Personal Protection Services,' Marko added.

'Yes,' she said, with a brief, broad smile, 'I did.'

Marko stood up, and walked to Jasmine.

He reached out, and untangled her hands from each other—although she hadn't even realised she'd been twisting and untwisting her fingers together until his touch halted her. He held both her hands gently, and waited while Jas slowly lifted her gaze from their joined clasp to meet with his.

'Dragi moj,' Marko said, so softly. 'I'm really sorry that this happened to you, and that, because you're helping me, it's happening again.'

'I'll be fine,' she said. 'I'm tough. I can handle it.'

'I know you will,' he said. Then he shook his head. 'Jasmine Gallagher, you are remarkable.'

Then he kissed her, as tears—for no reason Jas could fathom—made her throat feel tight and her eyes prickle.

When they broke apart, he spoke against her lips—just as Jas had spoken against his earlier. 'Thank you for trusting me.'

Jas closed her eyes. She *did* trust him.

Dragi moj.

It was a phrase that she *did* recognise—an endearment she'd looked up after hearing it between Lukas and Petra, and between other couples while she'd been in Vela Ada.

My dear one.

It was hardly an extravagant display of affection—Jas *knew* it was just Marko offering her comfort. And yet—he'd never called her that before, and those simple words…said so softly in Marko's delicious, dark accent…

They'd made her heart ache. And dream, just fleetingly, of so much more with Marko.

But, while she knew that she could trust him with her past, and that he would *never* do anything like what Stuart had done to her…

It wasn't photos or secrets that she feared when it came to the Prince standing before her.

What scared her was how she was going to stop herself from trusting him with her heart.

CHAPTER FOURTEEN

IT SEEMED SUCH a shame to wake her.

Marko sat on the edge of Jas's bed, fully dressed. He'd been up for hours, his whirling thoughts making it impossible to sleep.

For the first time in his life he'd used his royal status to be unreasonable—he'd woken Ivan up well before five a.m., and shortly afterwards a very sleepy Palace Communications Secretary had been driven through the palace gates.

A long, at times heated, conversation had then been had—and now Marko was satisfied with what was going to happen next.

He just needed Jasmine to approve.

As if she sensed the direction of his thoughts, Jas's eyes fluttered open. She'd fallen asleep in his arms, in her bathrobe, as they'd watched some action movie they'd both taken great glee in dismantling for copious inaccuracies.

'Why bring a SWAT team if the detectives are going to go in first?'

'That is not *how you hold that firearm.'*
'Are they really going to touch all that evidence?'
'Dobro jutro,' Jas said now.

Pillow creases on her cheek did nothing to distract from how gorgeous she looked—her hair tumbled across her pillow, and her eyes almost green in the early morning light.

'Good morning to you, too,' he said. *'Kako si?'*

She shook her head, laughing. 'Nope, I've got nothing. I've exhausted my grasp of your language.'

'How are you?' he tried again, his lips quirking.

'Ah,' she said, 'I *do* know that one.' She stretched expansively, reached her arms up above her head, so her fingers grazed against the bedhead. 'Fabulous,' she said, making the word as long and elastic as the movement of her body.

'I'm glad to hear that,' he said.

Jas seemed to register now that he was dressed, and must have seen something in his expression. She pulled herself up so she was sitting.

'What's wrong?' she asked.

'I've just heard that our legal team and the police have had no luck in tracking down the person or persons attempting to extort you.'

Jas shrugged, but he saw the flicker of disappointment in her expression. 'Isn't that what we expected?'

'Yes,' he said. 'But I'd hoped…'

She nodded. Yes, she'd hoped too. 'So we're going ahead with the press release today?'

'Yes,' Marko said. 'That's what I wanted to talk to you about.'

Jas looked at him curiously. They'd both already approved the content yesterday.

'I've changed the phrasing of the release, slightly,' Marko said. He handed the piece of paper he'd been holding to Jas.

She read through it carefully, occasionally flicking her gaze upwards to meet his.

'This is more than a slight change,' she said. 'The original press release was from the palace. This is from you.'

'There's something else,' Marko said. 'Rather than just releasing it, I'd like to make a video of me reading it, and release that instead.'

'Why?' Jas's tone was direct, almost accusatory. It surprised him.

'Because what happened to you a few years ago was not acceptable, and what's happening now is not acceptable. I think that message will be stronger if it comes from me personally, rather than with just the palace letterhead.'

Jas shook her head. 'You don't have to do that, Marko. I'll be out of the public eye in a few months' time. It's not like I'm really Vela Ada's future princess that you need to defend.'

He didn't understand her reaction. 'I know I don't have to do this. But I *want* to. Last night… I was so angry about it I couldn't sleep. I watched you sleeping in my arms and hated how helpless I felt.'

'I don't need you to protect me, Marko.'

Jas stood up and walked over to the window, pulling the curtains all the way open, so sunlight now flooded the room. Before the room had felt sleepy and fuzzy edged, now everything was hard and stark.

Marko didn't move from where he sat on the bed, giving her the space she seemed to need.

'But that's the thing, Jas,' he said. 'I can't protect you from stuff like this. Clearly, I *haven't*. And you didn't sign up for this—this *never* would've happened if you hadn't agreed to help me. I've put up with this rubbish my whole life, but to drag *you* into it, to drag my fiancée into it, and in this way… It crossed a line.'

Jas turned from the window to face him. She'd crossed her arms, and was hugging herself tightly. 'But I'm not really your fiancée.'

Her lips quirked upwards, but only momentarily.

'That doesn't matter. Why do you think I've never fallen—?'

He'd been thinking *married*, but he'd almost said *fallen in love.*

He mentally gave himself a shake. That didn't matter either.

'I've never addressed the gossip and lies published about myself before. The palace has a legal team to deal with the libellous, but anything simply fictional I've let slide. And in my silence I've created space for my grossly exaggerated Playboy Prince persona and I am not going to create space for the violation of your privacy in this way by yet more silence.' He held Jas's gaze unwaveringly as he spoke. 'A carefully worded press release in palace-speak is not good enough. I want anyone, anywhere in the world who considers publishing your photos to know that I, *personally*, will go after them should they do so. And I will do everything in my power to destroy them.'

For long seconds the room was completely silent.

Jasmine uncrossed her arms. 'Destroy seems rather a strong word,' she said, with half a grin. 'How exactly would you do that?'

But her smile did not reach her eyes, which gleamed with…unshed tears? He couldn't imagine Jas Gallagher crying.

'Details,' he said, with a wave of his hand. 'Believe me, I'd find a way.'

And he would.

He stood, and strode to stand before Jas.

'So?' he asked. 'Do you approve?'

She nodded, then tilted her chin upwards to look up at him. She'd blinked away any tears—or maybe they'd never existed.

'Just one thing,' she said. 'Can I do it with you?'

Marko smiled. 'I was hoping you'd say that.'

Jas and Marko filmed their statement in the Knight's Hall.

They sat together on a small baroque-style couch with an ornate, gold-leafed frame, with their hands linked together and rested casually on the red velvet upholstery as they each read from the teleprompter.

Marko was dressed in a charcoal suit, and Jas in an elegant cream boat-neck dress. Her hair and make-up were professionally styled and applied— and it all felt very formal for not even nine o'clock in the morning.

Marko spoke first in the Vela Ada dialect. Immediately afterwards, he repeated what he'd said in English.

Jas knew exactly what he was going to say, and yet, still, his words made her throat feel tight, and her fingers grip his more firmly.

Partly it was because, well…it was pretty damn confronting to be faced with the reality that immediately after this statement was released there was a high probability naked photos of her would end up in cyberspace.

If she thought about that too long she'd want to curl up in a hole somewhere and never face the light of day—or the judgment of Joe Public—ever again.

But the emotions she was feeling—embarrassment, regret—were losing a battle against the bubbling elation she felt about what they were doing.

Initially she'd balked when he'd told her his plans. She'd hated the idea of someone else fighting her battles for her. Of doubting her ability to look after herself.

But as he'd stood before her in her room, in front of that amazing view of Vela Ada, she'd slowly realised that Marko wasn't trying to fight anything *for* her, he wanted to go into battle *beside* her.

And as hard as she might have tried to convince herself—at first—that he would do this for anyone, she didn't actually believe that.

For all their talk of fun and no expectations—and she *still* had no expectations—she knew that right now there was a connection between them. Right now she had Marko beside her in every sense of the word. And right now, that was exactly what she needed.

Marko was speaking of his long history and poor relationship with the media. Of his journey from anger to apathy when it came to how he'd been portrayed, and his regret that he had not made a stand earlier.

He spoke, heartbreakingly, of the cruelty of being photographed during the worst time of his life as his father died—of having images of his grief only a click away, and impossible to escape.

'You may say this is the price I pay for being a prince, but, as grateful as I am for my privileged life, it is still *my* life, and I have the same rights to privacy as everyone else. Just as Jasmine does, too.'

Marko shifted his gaze from the teleprompter to meet her own.

'And, of course, this is not about me.'

Marko squeezed her hand as Jas steadied her gaze on the teleprompter.

'Several years ago,' she began, 'I sent some naked photos of myself to my then boyfriend, and later, without my permission, he shared those photos with others.' Jas swallowed. 'I want to make it clear that even now I do not regret taking those photos. I am not ashamed of them. However, they are personal photos taken with a very specific audience in mind. An audience I *chose*. I never wished for anyone to ever see them without my permission, and when that happened it was awful—and the way I felt I wouldn't wish on anyone. I made a mistake in putting my trust in a man who did not deserve it. I do not regret taking those photos, but I do not want anyone else to see them.' She paused. 'Should these photos be released, I am putting my trust in you. I am trusting you to respect my privacy, in the way that everyone on this planet should have their privacy respected.'

Jas repeated her statement in carefully practised Slavic.

And then—her part was done.

She was still being filmed as Marko finished their statement, so she couldn't relax, as such. And yet, she definitely did feel as if a weight had been lifted.

A weight she'd been carrying for years—and that insidious voice that had blamed herself for what had happened, that had told her she was stupid, naïve, and blinded by love, had finally been silenced.

She'd known, logically, that she'd been the victim. She'd known that if she *had* decided to pursue charges against Stuart the law was on her side.

But that hadn't mattered in the end. Everyone she'd told had been shocked she'd taken the photos, and had struggled to understand why she'd done it. Only Marko hadn't cared about any of that. He hadn't judged her. Instead, he'd understood her.

'I ask you to remember that she did not choose to fall in love with a prince. She fell in love with me.'

Marko's words—unexpected and definitely *not* part of the script—dragged Jas's attention back to the man beside her. She met his gaze, confused and disoriented. *Why say that?*

But he answered the question in her eyes with a kiss—soft and brief.

When his lips lifted from hers, the camera crew started talking quickly, and Marko got to his feet, reaching out a hand for her.

He chatted to the woman behind the camera for a minute, before turning to Jas.

'Let's leave them to edit,' he said. 'I hope you don't mind my ad-lib at the end. The crew loved it though, thought it was a nice touch.'

A nice touch?

Jas knew she shouldn't feel so disconcerted by a sentence so in keeping with their supposed engagement.

To hear talk of *love* now, just as she was finally letting go of her own self-flagellation, which had been so closely linked to her—again supposed—love she'd felt for Stuart, had left her flustered.

She'd thought she'd loved Stuart, but she realised now much of her pain had been that of betrayal, and not of lost love. Love had never existed between them, no matter how badly Jas might have wanted it to.

But with Marko...

No.

That was impossible. She'd known him only weeks. She'd lived thirty years without telling a man that she loved him. Without truly falling in love. She knew that now.

So to fall in love with Marko, a man with no interest in a relationship, let alone love...

No. To fall for Marko was a self-fulfilling prophecy of pain and disappointment. As she'd known right from the very beginning, Jasmine Gallagher was no princess. Without the circumstances that had thrown them together, Marko would never even have noticed her in a crowd.

He might have noticed her now, and they might have some sort of a connection...but to extrapolate that to be love would be as naïve as the trust she'd placed in Stuart.

Marko had led her to the wide hallway outside the Knight's Hall. He was looking at her curiously.

'Jas—'

'I'm just going to go up to my room,' she said quickly, not quite meeting his gaze. 'I'd better call my mum before the video goes out.'

'I'll see you at lunch?' he asked.

She shook her head. 'No. I—' A beat passed. She'd been going to say she was feeling unwell, but she didn't want to lie. 'I think I need some time alone, if that's okay,' she said. 'These last few days have been...overwhelming.'

In so many different ways.

Marko frowned. 'Are you sure?' he said. 'I don't like leaving you alone—'

'Marko,' Jas said, much more sharply than she intended. 'I am *fine*. I promise. I just need some space.'

Marko nodded just as sharply as she'd spoken. 'Let me know if you need me,' he said abruptly.

Then he walked off down the hallway, to where, Jas had no idea.

Leaving Jas to head for her room.

Just like a few days earlier, she told herself that having some space was a good idea.

Back then, she'd been worried about blurring the lines of their relationship—from fun to serious. From superficial to sharing their deepest secrets.

But those lines had now been erased.

Let me know if you need me, he'd said.

And that was the thing, of course.

She didn't need Marko. She just needed to remind herself of that.

CHAPTER FIFTEEN

'*SHE DID NOT choose to fall in love with a prince. She fell in love with me...*'

Why had he said that?

Marko stood beside Jas later that evening, in the historic Vela Ada City Hall. They had yet another event, this time honouring some of Vela Ada's most generous citizens—people who had dedicated their lives selflessly to others. Foster carers, disability campaigners, philanthropists—it was a diverse group of very good people, and a heartening reminder that such people existed, given that it had taken mere minutes after their videoed statement was released for Jas's photos to end up all over the Internet.

The police and the palace were managing the situation as best they could. Jasmine was handling it brilliantly.

She'd emerged from her room appearing refreshed, and certainly without that almost panicked look she'd had after they'd finished filming.

She'd hidden it well, but he'd noted it the moment it had appeared—which was the moment he'd mentioned her—apparent—love for him.

He shouldn't have gone off script, but at the time it had felt right.

While videoing the statement had helped to channel some of his anger at the whole situation, it hadn't helped to abate it. And much of that anger was still directed at himself. This *was* his fault. As he'd said—Jas hadn't chosen this.

But mentioning love, even faux love, even if his intent was to show that Jasmine had done nothing to deserve any of this, was a mistake.

He should've known, given his own reaction to Jas's joke about them being 'madly in love' when they'd been surprised by that cleaner in a passionate clinch. He still couldn't work out how he'd felt—other than he hadn't found the joke amusing, and he didn't really know why.

Also, he hadn't allowed himself to think too much about it. He wasn't a man who had ever spent much time reflecting on *love*, in any context.

So why mention love, especially on camera?

He could lie and tell himself it was all part of the role he was playing—of a loving, concerned, protective fiancé.

But he wasn't really playing that role. He was

genuinely concerned, genuinely protective—even if Jas insisted she didn't need him to be, and was probably right. The only thing false about the situation had been the fiancée bit. And the bit about Jas loving him.

She was in sparkling, princess form tonight. She'd grown into her role over the weeks, and now she effortlessly charmed everyone she met. Even tonight, as Vela Ada buzzed about the 'photo scandal', she was flawless. Dressed in a form-fitting deep red dress and holding a glass of pink champagne, she chatted easily beside him. It was Marko who was discombobulated.

The gentleman who had been speaking to him, Marko realised belatedly, had disappeared at some point as Marko had been lost in his own thoughts. Jas bumped her shoulder against his arm, and glanced up at him, asking him a wordless question: *You okay?*

He nodded.

Why do you think I've never fallen in love?

He'd almost asked that question of Jas earlier that day, and now he asked it of himself.

He knew the answer. Since the very first girl he'd kissed, he'd known he couldn't bring someone he loved into the suffocating, scrutinised life of a royal. He would not allow the woman he loved to be defined by her relationship with him—to become nothing but the royal title that marriage to Prince Marko would bestow.

To love him, and to marry him, was to lose too much of herself. He would not wish the way his life was invaded, and judged, and labelled on his worst enemy, let alone the woman he loved.

Yet—here he stood. Beside a woman who had had her privacy violated in a way that was more horrendous than *any* he had experienced. Yet she still stood beside him.

Was that due to her contract and hefty fee?

Even considering that possibility felt like a betrayal.

No, he knew Jas Gallagher. As he watched her now she straightened her shoulders and smiled. She was every inch a strong, resilient woman. And that was no façade.

Something—a sudden movement—caught Marko's eye.

A split second later, an exclamation from the surrounding crowd followed:

'*Nož! Nož!* He's got a knife!'

And then Marko saw it—a flash of a silver blade, the whites of the knuckles of the man that gripped it fiercely.

The movement of that blade towards him.

THE PRINCE'S FAKE FIANCÉE

Instinct took over—his army training allowing him to instantly assess the threat, to move to disarm the—

But then, in a blur of a jet-black suit, the man was gone, tackled to the ground by Simon. In the same instant Jas had her arm around him, guiding him into a crouch. At his other hip materialised another person from Jas's team, and together they ran for the exit—an exit Marko hadn't even been aware existed, but Jas clearly did, guiding him there with total confidence.

The whole time, she was barking instructions to her team.

It felt wrong—totally wrong—to be fleeing from a threat.

He wanted to stay—he wanted to make sure the threat was disabled. He wanted to assist with clearing the room, with ensuring no other threats lurked, waiting.

But that wasn't his role.

He wasn't Lieutenant Colonel Marko Pavlovic today, and he certainly wasn't a bodyguard.

He was the target.

Now through the door they ran down service steps, three pairs of feet somehow almost perfectly in sync with each other. Jas's feet were in stockings only, her spiky heels obviously discarded for haste.

The other bodyguard paused at a heavy access door, talking urgently into his earpiece. Then the door was opened from outside, where two more from the team waited and then—perfectly timed—their car arrived. Moments later he and Jas were in the back seat, and well before anyone could consider details like seat belts they were off—just as Marko heard sirens approaching in the distance.

'You okay?' Jas asked finally.

He nodded. 'Perfectly.'

From the front seat, Scott turned. 'Suspect arrested,' he said. 'Simon is fine.'

Beside him, Jas breathed a heavy sigh. 'Great job, everyone,' she said.

Then she turned to Marko, her mouth kicking up into a triumphant grin. 'Now that,' she said, 'was a lot of fun.'

'Fun?'

It was several hours later, and Jas lay beside Marko in his bed. He was propped up on one elbow, his gaze trained on hers.

The room was lit only by a single lamp, all that had been needed for doing what had seemed logical after a threat to Marko's life: make love.

No. Jas corrected herself. *Have sex.*

The night had been a blur after their escape from

City Hall and then the necessary reports to police. They'd barely had a chance to talk.

Jas smiled up at him. 'You know exactly what I meant. You do so much training—for months and years—for *exactly* those moments. And for it to all come together so perfectly…yes, it was awesome.'

'I hate that I put you in danger.'

Jas snorted. 'Are you serious?'

'No,' he said, 'hear me out. What if that guy had gone for you?'

'He wouldn't have got near me. I could've disarmed him, but I wouldn't have needed to. My team was onto it.' Jas narrowed her eyes as she studied him. 'It is literally my job to deal with this stuff, Marko.'

'But it isn't your job to be the target. With me you're a target.'

She shook her head. 'I wasn't. That guy was one of Senator Božić's supporters. He wasn't angry with me, he was angry at your brother—and you, as his proxy. Not me.'

'But another time it could be you.'

She raised an eyebrow. 'I've known that from the start. That's why we have bodyguards, Marko. It's why you employed my team.'

Marko rolled, moving his body until he was above her, his hands tangled in her hair.

The intensity of Marko's gaze shocked Jas. The sudden intimacy—the way he was holding her so gently, his thumbs tracing her jaw and cheekbones—made her breath catch.

He kept his weight mostly off her, but they still touched all the way along her body—breast to chest, hip to hip, skin to skin.

'What if something had happened to you, Jas?' he asked.

She held her tongue when it would've been so easy to retort that she could look after herself.

She knew that wasn't what Marko wanted to hear right now.

So she remained silent, letting him speak.

'I could've stopped that guy,' Marko insisted.

Jas nodded. She knew that.

'And I understand that it isn't my role. But I *hated* how helpless I felt. How I was reduced to being a helpless prince you had to protect.'

Jas narrowed her eyes. 'You'd better not think it's your job as a man to protect me,' she said. 'Or that it's not my job to protect you.'

'No,' he said, with the slightest quirk of his lips. 'It's our job to protect each other.'

Oh. Those words did those funny flip-floppy things to her heart.

She didn't like that, and so she started talking in

her no-nonsense work voice: 'If you want a more active role in your protection we can probably involve you more closely. Engage you in our tactics—'

'That isn't what I meant, Jas,' he said gently.

He bridged the gap between them, pressing his mouth to hers. As were all their kisses, it was sweet, and sexy…but this one was also almost frighteningly intimate…

Jas wrenched her lips away. 'What did you mean, then?'

Marko held her gaze again. In the muted light his expression was like nothing she'd seen before—intense but open. As if, for the first time, he was revealing everything to her.

Then he rolled away.

Jas propped herself up onto her elbow to study him.

But his gaze now was unreadable.

Jas considered pushing him for an answer. Part of her needed to—she *needed* to know what he was thinking, she needed to make sense of the ache in her heart and the whirling in her head…

But the other part of her felt the adrenalin that had kept her buzzing drain rapidly out of her system. Suddenly, she was so very tired.

She crawled to Marko, wrapping her arms around his chest, and burying her head in his shoulder.

She breathed in the clean scent of his skin, and listened to the beat of his heart beneath her ear.

'Jasmine?'

Only now did she allow the reality of tonight to settle on her shoulders. Only now did she make tonight about something other than a successful job.

Until right now, it had been fun. It had been about her team, and about their successful extraction of their principal. She'd been all arrogant bluster and cocky satisfaction.

But as she listened to Marko breathe, she finally let herself embrace the fear that it was her job to compartmentalise.

Not fear for herself, or fear of their attacker tonight.

'What if something had happened to you, Marko?' she said, oh, so softly, against the rise and fall of his chest.

CHAPTER SIXTEEN

MARKO CANCELLED ALL royal engagements the following day.

Instead, in a single car, Jas and Marko went to the beach. To Marko's isolated, private beach.

This time, he was prepared. They had an oversized beach umbrella, colourful plush towels and a gourmet picnic basket complete with wines from a Vela Ada vineyard. It was a gorgeous day, the sky clear except for the slightest wisps of cloud, and the ocean all perfectly still shades of blue.

After falling asleep last night with Jas curled against his body, they'd barely spoken. Marko had woken before Jas and gone for a long, punishing run. When he'd returned, Jas had already headed to her *salon* to work. Although when he'd interrupted her shortly after to invite her to the beach, she'd accepted immediately.

Maybe she understood, or shared, his need to escape?

But escape from what, exactly?

Even here—in this perfect, private, place—Marko hadn't relaxed.

He lay on his towel, wearing nothing but his board shorts, trying to enjoy the beat of the sun against his skin, and the sound of the waves lapping against the shore.

But it wasn't working.

At his side lay Jas. She was wearing a green and white polka-dot bikini, a broad-brimmed white straw hat and oversized sunglasses, and held a book in her hands that she appeared completely absorbed by.

But—her body seemed tense too. Or was he just overthinking things?

He didn't know what was wrong with him. This didn't feel like a normal reaction to an attempt on his life—especially as he'd never actually felt his life was in danger.

Last night…

Last night his brain had been busy with thoughts of Jas, and today all he'd wanted to do was spend time with her. Only her—no one else.

So here they were. But things between them weren't how he wanted them to be. He was tense, and she *was* tense. Out of the corner of his eye he saw her bouncing her foot, just slightly, against the sand. She was fidgeting, and Jas didn't fidget.

He should probably talk to her. Talk to her properly, not the slightly stilted small talk they'd managed in the car.

But last night they *had* been talking, and he'd stopped. She'd stopped, too.

What he wanted between them, right now, was for it to feel easy. But last night hadn't felt easy. It had been the opposite of easy.

Now wasn't easy either.

He stood quickly, shoving himself up from the sand.

'Marko?'

He didn't look at her. 'Just going for a swim,' he said.

In the water—which annoyed him by not being bracingly cold and rough but instead warm and languid—he immediately leapt into a powerful freestyle, heading for the horizon.

He swam and swam and swam—heading well past the boundary of the cove. When he finally stopped to tread water, the ocean had pushed him slightly around the edge of a peninsula, so now he could no longer see their private beach. In fact, where he swam now, he could see nobody. There was not one boat, not one person on the shore, nothing.

He lay back in the water, and stared up at the almost cloudless sky.

What was up with him?

Jasmine Gallagher.

The answer was so obvious; she'd been all that filled his thoughts—as he'd slept, as he'd run, and as he'd swum.

Over the past few days the concept of their relationship being fun or casual or easy had become farcical. With Jas he'd shared more than he'd ever shared with any other woman—but what did that mean?

What did it mean that last night he'd felt a fear that he'd never before experienced—the fear of losing the woman he…

What?

Loved?

No. It was too impossible.

Even considering the possibility seemed ridiculous. They'd been together only weeks, known each other not much longer.

But even if it was possible, it didn't actually matter.

Because—after last night—he knew, inarguably, that he'd been right to never drag a woman into his life in any permanent way. Jas's privacy had been irretrievably invaded because of him, and last night she could've been *killed* because of him.

That wasn't acceptable.

Marko turned back onto his belly, and swam back the way he'd come. As he entered the cove he saw Jas standing at the end of the narrow jetty that stretched out from the far end of the rocky beach, and where he and Lukas had fished what felt like a hundred years ago.

So he swam to Jas.

At the wooden jetty, he hauled himself out of the water to stand beside her.

He realised, belatedly, that she was glaring at him, and her hands were placed firmly at her hips.

Then, before he had any idea what she intended, said hands were pressed forcefully against his chest—and, throwing her entire weight behind it, she shoved Marko straight back into the ocean.

They hit the water almost simultaneously, then surfaced less than a metre apart.

'What the hell, Jas?' he exclaimed.

She was treading water furiously, her hair slicked back, and her hazel eyes sparked with anger.

'What the hell, *Marko*?' she retorted. 'Someone tried to kill you yesterday, and *you* just went for a swim and *disappeared*. How do you think I felt when I looked up from my book and I couldn't see you?'

'I wasn't in any danger, Jas,' he said, attempting a soothing tone.

'But I didn't know that!' she snapped. 'How could you be so bloody—?'

Her voice cracked, and she looked away, her eyes squinting in the bright sunlight.

He swam closer to her, reaching out to brush her fingers beneath the water with his own.

He'd scared her. Properly scared her. His brave, strong Jasmine.

'I'm sorry,' he said. 'I didn't think.'

She snorted. *'Obviously.'*

She turned and swam the short distance back to the jetty. As he watched, she pulled herself out of the water, and then perched herself at the very end of the structure so her toes just dipped into the sea.

He followed suit behind her, and a minute later he was sitting beside her, the sun quickly evaporating the sheen of water from their skin.

Jas didn't think she'd ever been as scared as she'd felt when she'd realised Marko wasn't in the cove.

She'd raced down the jetty, searching the water desperately for him, while shouting his name.

Two from her team were waiting for them in

the car above the dunes as Marko had insisted that they be allowed to relax in privacy. After last night, Jas had been too emotionally exhausted to argue. Plus, no one knew about this beach, and they'd made sure they weren't followed. But as her feet had drummed against the wooden jetty boards she'd lambasted herself for her stupidity. If something had happened to Marko…

But then she'd seen him, swimming strong, easy strokes as he swam into view from beyond the cove.

It was only now, with Marko sitting beside her on the jetty, that her breathing returned to normal.

'What's going on, Marko?' she asked abruptly.

Suddenly it seemed pointless to pretend any longer.

'Between us?' he asked.

She knew he knew what she meant, so she didn't bother to respond. All day things had been weird between them. Last night had been intense. And, it appeared, a turning point.

At least for Jasmine.

'I don't know what's going on,' Marko said finally. 'This isn't what I expected when I kissed you at *Mjesto za Ljubljenje*. This is…more.'

More.

He shifted beside her so his body was angled

towards hers. She did the same, tipping her chin upwards so that she could meet his gaze.

He was as handsome as always, even under the harsh Mediterranean sun that made his eyes crinkle at the corners.

'More what?' she said bluntly.

He laughed and shook his head. 'You're not making this easy, Jas.'

'*This* isn't easy,' she pointed out.

'No,' he conceded. 'This…*us* isn't easy.' Jas watched his Adam's apple as he swallowed. 'I've never felt like this with another woman, Jas,' he said. 'I know that.'

Jas nodded.

'What do you think is going on?' he asked, after a while.

She shrugged. 'Something that I want to last longer than my contract,' she said simply. 'So I need you to let me know if that's what you want, too, as otherwise…'

Here her bravado faded away.

'Otherwise?' he prompted.

'Otherwise,' she said, channelling her sensible, direct self, 'I think it's better if we end it now. I had the last man I thought I loved break my trust and my heart. I'm not going to wait around for that to happen again if it's only inevitable.'

She was making it sound like if she walked away now it was 'no harm, no foul'—but the ache already in her heart told her very, very differently.

But Marko didn't need to know that.

It's our job to protect each other.

If he really believed that, if he really felt that, then...

'The last man you thought you loved?' Marko said. 'Love?'

His expression wasn't shocked, exactly. More thoughtful. As if turning the idea over in his head.

'Maybe,' Jas said. 'One day.'

Like, possibly, yesterday.

But Jas wasn't allowing herself to think about that too much. And she certainly wasn't going to tell Marko.

She might have let her dormant dreams of love and happiness and rainbows bubble towards the surface—but she hadn't allowed them to bubble over. She'd learnt something, at least, from Stuart. Her trust, and her heart, weren't so easily offered up now.

If Marko loved her—or *could* love her—she'd know soon enough.

It's our job to protect each other.

So she needed to know: were they a team, or not?

'Love...' Marko repeated.

'Yes,' Jas said firmly. *'Love.'*

His gaze drifted out towards the horizon. 'I don't know, Jas. I've never been in a long-term relationship. I've literally never brought a woman home to the palace, or to meet my mother, until you. This is different, it's unfamiliar—'

Jas pushed herself up to her feet, suddenly annoyed. 'Marko, this isn't about the past. Hell, if we're going to dwell on the past you'd think I've got a pretty good reason to be cautious, don't you think? Yet I've got the guts to tell you how I'm feeling, and you can't even answer a simple question. *What do you think's going on between us, Marko?'* She looked up at the sky, the sun blinding her. 'I need you to tell me.'

Jas squeezed her eyes shut against the glare, suddenly realising there was no 'maybe' or 'one day' when it came to Marko. She loved him.

The realisation made her throat tight and her eyes sting.

When she opened her eyes, Marko was also on his feet. She met his gaze, strong and steady.

His was steady too. No looking away from her now.

'I'm a prince, Jasmine. My life…the life you would have with me… I don't think you understand what you'd be getting into. I don't think it's fair to—'

'You don't think I'd understand?' Jas said, furious now. 'Don't patronise me. The last month I've been literally beside you every step of your royal life. I've survived the paparazzi, an assassination attempt and a nude photo scandal. I think I get it, Marko.'

'But it wasn't real, Jas.'

Shocked, Jas turned on her heel, unable to be close to him right now.

How could he say that, when the past few weeks had felt more real than anything she'd ever experienced?

Halfway down the jetty his hand closed around her wrist. When she tried to tug away, he pulled her effortlessly against his chest, wrapping his arms tightly around her.

'I'm so sorry, *dragi moj*,' he said into her hair. 'I didn't mean it like that. The way I feel for you *is* real, I promise you. What we've had is real. But this whole time you've had an end date. You've known it's not for ever. It's different when it is. When you take on the burden of the world's scrutiny for the rest of your life.'

For a long moment Jas just stood in his arms, her cheek pressed against his chest. She kept her eyes squeezed shut as she listened to his heartbeat, and sank against the rise and fall of his breathing.

Then, she stepped away.

'That's just an excuse, Marko,' she said. 'I have a life in Australia and a business that takes me around the world. This stuff is complicated, I get it. But it's surmountable, to me. Nothing is insurmountable for the man I love.'

There. She'd done it. She'd said it.

Her declaration of love seemed to hang between them, their world silent beyond the murmur of the waves.

Then he shook his head. 'It's not an excuse, Jas.'

She put her hands on her hips. 'Is it love, then—this thing between us? This thing you can't explain? Do you love me?'

Marko's gaze searched her face, tracing her eyes, her nose, her lips.

Jas kept her gaze steady, even as her heart drummed against her chest, and her throat felt so tight she could barely breathe.

'I don't know, Jas,' he said finally as Jas desperately tried to work out what was going on behind his eyes. His expression was unreadable, but his gaze…

Then, he took a deep breath, as if he'd made a decision. 'No, Jas,' he said. 'I don't think it's love.'

* * *

Jas hadn't said a word.

Instead, she'd let *his* words hang between them, long enough that they began to feel tangible—as if Marko could reach out and snatch them back.

I don't think it's love.

But he didn't take the words back. He just stood there and watched, and waited, as Jas's bravado began to crumble.

But only for an instant.

Of course, Jas wasn't one to crumble. She was a fighter, his Jasmine. That was what she'd been doing, here on the jetty. Fighting. For him, for herself. For them.

His Jasmine.

She wasn't, of course. He had no right to even think such a thing as he watched her walk away from him. Her pace regular and determined. No more crumbling.

But also, no more fighting.

She'd fought for him, but he'd made his decision.

It was the right decision, for him. For both of them.

He knew that, absolutely, as the sun beat down on his bare skin, and his toes gripped the splintering boards of the jetty.

He followed her, but a while later.

His pace was slow. His limbs felt heavy—as if all the fight had seeped out of him.

Which made sense. The fight was over.

But then, why did he feel as if he'd lost?

CHAPTER SEVENTEEN

Three days later

MARKO SAT BENEATH vines heavy with grapes, a glass of wine in his hand.

Lukas sat beside him, his mostly untouched lunch on the table before him. They both stared out across the olive groves. Inside, their mother was attempting to teach Petra how to make her secret version of *crni rižoto*—black cuttlefish risotto—and occasionally their bursts of laughter would travel outside to where Marko and Lukas sat in silence.

It wasn't an uncomfortable silence. Lukas was still fatigued from his latest round of chemotherapy, and he'd explained to Marko last time they'd spoken that he often found it hard to follow conversations—he was just too exhausted to pay careful attention.

But that suited Marko today, to just sit here and not make conversation. And to let his mind drift. To not *think* too much.

The past few days had been a blur. After the disaster of their day on the beach, he and Jas had returned to the palace. Jas had been adamant she'd continue her role as his fiancée, although Marko had disagreed. Continuing their lie seemed ludicrous now, although Jas had eventually convinced him that 'breaking up' was the worst thing to do given the turmoil and scandal of the past few days. Vela Ada and the palace needed their relationship to appear solid and unbreakable.

Yes, but what did Jasmine need? What did he need?

But he hadn't asked those questions, and they'd instead avoided each other in the palace, and then both acted their backsides off when they'd headed to open a new oncology ward named after Marko's father.

But spending time with Jas had been excruciating. To stop himself from touching her in all the ways that had become second nature—guiding her through doorways with a hand at her waist, holding her hand, standing just close enough so their arms brushed together…

Although he'd held her hand to help her out of their car when they'd arrived at the hospital. And that had almost been worse—to touch her, but know it was only for show…

This morning, Ivan had brought a message to him. Jas would like to return home for a week for her mother's birthday.

He didn't doubt it was her mother's birthday, but he also knew she'd had no plans to go home for it until today. His instinct had been to go talk to her, to tell her to take all the time she needed. And that he was so sorry. So sorry he couldn't give her what she needed. So sorry he couldn't love her.

Instead he'd sent Ivan back with his approval, and not long after he'd watched from the terrace as she'd left—with her bodyguards—for the airport, in one of the palace cars. Behind tinted windows he couldn't even see her, and briefly he'd fought the instinct to race down the stairs and go after her. And...

What, exactly?

Nothing had changed. He still knew he'd made the right decision.

'Marko?'

Marko blinked, turning to face Lukas. Lukas was looking at him like someone who had been trying to get his attention for some time.

'Sorry,' he said. 'Just thinking.'

'About Jasmine?'

Marko took a long sip of his wine. 'Pardon me?'

Lukas grinned. 'Come on,' he said, 'I'm sick, not stupid. Obviously there's trouble in paradise.'

Marko shook his head. 'Everything's fine. I thought you didn't like talking much at the moment.'

'And I thought you didn't like lying to your brother, and you've got pretty good at that.'

Marko put his glass down on the wooden table. 'I don't know what you're talking about.'

Lukas sighed. 'I know that you're not really engaged to Jasmine. I suspected right from the start—it seemed exactly the type of crazy thing you would do. Petra disagreed with me and was positive it was all real—until you both visited here, and then she worked it out, too. But we weren't going to say anything, because, honestly—it was a genius idea. No one cares about their King having a serious illness when they've got a new princess to get excited about.'

'Glad to be of service,' Marko said drily. There was no point at all in denying any of it. It had been years since he and Lukas had been close, but once they'd shared everything. Lukas still knew him better than almost anyone. Except Jas…

He mentally gave himself a shake. No, he wasn't going there.

'You have been,' Lukas said, his expression serious. 'I know you hate all the royal stuff, and, honestly, I didn't know how you'd manage stepping in for me. But you've been brilliant, exactly the Prince that Vela Ada needed.'

'Except for the photo scandal, and the assassination attempt—'

Lukas shrugged. 'You couldn't have responded better to either. You and Jasmine have captured the hearts of everyone. Vela Ada has fallen in love with you.'

Love.

That damn word again.

'It's remarkable, really,' Lukas said. 'How real your relationship has appeared.'

Marko met Lukas's gaze. He knew what his brother was thinking; he knew his brother thought there was more to him and Jasmine than a contract.

Marko stood up. 'She's an incredible—'

He was going to say *actress*, but found he couldn't.

Instead, he tried again: 'She's incredible,' he said simply.

But it's not real.

Turned out he couldn't say that, either.

Marko then walked away, almost jogging really, down the slight slope to the edge of the olive grove, not wanting to discuss any of this with his brother.

A breeze rustled the leaves that surrounded him as he strode between the olive trees.

Lukas didn't call out to him, but Marko had known he wouldn't.

After a while, he did break into a jog. Then a run.

But no matter how fast he ran, he couldn't escape from what he knew, and what he'd always known.

What he'd had with Jas was real. He'd told her that, on that jetty, but at the time it hadn't been enough.

This morning, it hadn't been enough. He'd convinced himself it wasn't.

But now, he wasn't so sure.

Ainslie, Canberra

Jas's mum hadn't actually organised anything for her birthday. On her birthday, Jas had simply arrived, unannounced, on her mother's doorstep—managing to avoid the Australian media thanks to a private plane and the excellent organisation of the palace and Australian diplomatic staff.

She'd now been here two days and although she hadn't left the house—and poor Simon and Scott were absolutely bored out of their brains—it still seemed the media were clueless. And for as long as that lasted, Jas was eternally grateful.

Because all she felt capable of doing right now was sleeping and watching romantic comedies in her teenage room.

She'd also cried for some time on her mother's shoulder—and promptly broken her confidentiality contract by telling her everything.

But it had helped to do so. So much.

It was Friday night, and her mum was hosting her book club in her blue weatherboard cottage. Jas was hiding in her room, as she absolutely knew that her mum's friends wouldn't be able to keep her presence a secret. They wouldn't go to the media, obviously, but they'd definitely tell one of their kids, and then...

Anyway, the upshot was she was stuck in her room. Her mum had brought her a platter of cheese and biscuits, and she'd curled herself up on her bed in her oldest, comfiest jeans and a T-shirt from a gig she went to when she was seventeen. Simon and Scott were sharing the tiny spare room, and the whole situation was ridiculous if Jas thought too much about it.

About halfway through her movie, there was a sharp knock at the front door. Her mum's house was small, and every sound travelled from one end of it to the other.

Consequently, Jas also heard the sound of the

book club ladies' voices rising, and then—a deep male voice.

Jas slid off her bed and was brushing the crumbs from her clothes as her mum knocked on her bedroom door.

'Jas?' her mum said. 'You have a visitor.'

Jas smiled a tight smile as she followed her mum down the hallway. Immediately behind her were her bodyguards—both probably relieved to be able to leave their room.

Her mum only had a single, small living area—an open-plan kitchen, dining area and lounge.

Currently, it was full.

The book-club ladies were spread between the kitchen and lounge, each with a champagne glass and an inquisitive expression. With her and her bodyguards adding to the space, it was definitely crowded, and that was before Jas included the person that everyone was staring at—Prince Marko of Vela Ada. Who currently stood beside her mother's overcrowded hat stand, and in front of a framed piece of Jas's primary school artwork.

She'd missed him.

That was her first thought when his gaze locked on hers.

He was dressed as if he'd come straight from a

plane, in jeans, T-shirt and sneakers and with tired smudges under his eyes.

He still looked gorgeous.

Behind him, beyond the still-open front door, were the rest of her team.

'Jas,' he said—and to hear his voice again made her shiver. 'I'm sorry.'

Jas took a long, deep breath. Then walked over to him, and grabbed his hand. She tugged him past the book club, past her mother—and her mother's concerned expression—and straight past Simon and Scott.

'No one is to follow us,' she said firmly.

Then she led Marko down the hallway, and outside.

Outside there was a simple patio, paved with recycled bricks that Jas and her mum had laid a decade earlier. A liquid amber provided shade during the day—but now, at night, its canopy of branches simply acted like a veil between them and the star-sparkled sky.

Jas dropped Marko's hand.

'Why are you here?' she asked.

'I needed to see you,' he said. 'And I needed to tell you something.'

Jas waited.

'I told you once that I hated the palace. Do you remember?'

She nodded. Yes, back when they'd first had breakfast together.

'But, of course, it was never about the palace itself, but who I was when I was there. At the palace, I'm Prince Marko. I'm not a senior military officer, I'm not a man with his own hopes and dreams and I'm certainly not a man with his own private life. I'm a prince, and that role is one I've never felt comfortable playing.'

Jas's eyes had adjusted to the darkness—not that she needed to be able to see to feel the intensity of his gaze.

'I've spent most of my life rebelling against the expectations of my family and Vela Ada, and hating the scrutiny I've been under my whole entire life. I've been judged, and found wanting, for as long as I can remember.'

'Marko—' Jas began, but he shook his head, silencing her.

'I may now complain about it, but I've been complicit in the lie of the Playboy Prince, hiding behind that façade rather than working out who I *actually* am. Not just who I am perceived to be. With you, Jasmine Gallagher, there's never been a façade. You've never treated me as anything but the man you see in front of you. You see me, you saw me…with you I'm just Marko, and what I had with you is about as real as anything I've ever experienced in my life. Even though we were only together because of a lie.'

Jas wanted to reach for him, but she kept her hands still, twisting her fingers in the fabric of her jeans instead.

'I've never had a serious relationship, Jas, because I've told myself I would never bring someone into a life I hated—a life of scrutiny and judgment. The past few weeks, this belief has been seemingly vindicated—after all, what sort of monster would I be to drag a woman into a life where her privacy is violated, and her life is under threat?' He swallowed. 'That's what I was telling myself that day on the jetty, Jas. I held onto it—onto what you quite rightly called an excuse—and held onto it tightly, right up until you flew back home to Australia.'

'What changed?' Jas asked, trying her best to tamp down the butterflies beginning to flutter in her belly. What was Marko saying?

'I found out Lukas knew from the start that our engagement was a lie.'

Jas gasped, but Marko just grinned.

'No, it's fine. No one else knows, except Petra. And probably my mum.'

Oh, God. But now was not the time to worry about all her lies to royalty.

'But it got me thinking, Jas, about what else I've been lying about. Like, for example, the lie I was telling myself that my decision to let you walk away was about *protecting* you. When it was never about that. It was about protecting myself. All these years I've told myself that I'd never drag someone I loved into a world I hated, but really— I think maybe I was just scared that no one would genuinely love me enough to look past all that. To put up with the paparazzi, and having their lives turned upside down—for me. For Marko, not Prince Marko.

'Or,' he continued, 'maybe I just hadn't met the right person.'

He stepped closer to her, but now he looked unsure. For the first time, ever, Jas saw uncertainty in Marko's gaze.

'Jasmine Gallagher,' he said, in his delicious, deep accent, 'I love you. I still don't know for sure if you'll want to run away from life as a princess in a few more weeks, or months or years…but I love you. So I need to trust that you might love me enough to stay.'

Jas reached out, lacing each of her hands with his, in an echo of the first time they'd touched as they'd walked into the Knight's Hall that very first night together.

Still, his touch made her shiver.

'I love you, Marko,' she said. 'I love the man you are: a man of strength, and loyalty and integrity. I don't care about the prince stuff, I just know I love *you*, and that's all that matters to me. You've taught me to believe in love again, to trust in love again. And I promise you, I'm not going anywhere.'

She stood on her tiptoes to kiss him, and instantly he was dragging her close, and kissing her until she was incapable of thinking, and certainly incapable of remembering she was in her mum's backyard. For long minutes her world was Marko, and the incredible, extraordinary way he made her feel.

When they finally broke apart, breathing heavily, they just stood there smiling at each other.

'It probably wouldn't be very polite of me to whisk you back to my hotel without properly introducing myself to your mother and her friends.'

'No,' Jas said, grinning. 'Not very kingly at all. Definitely not the behaviour of a prince.'

She reached up to pull him down for another

kiss, then whispered against his lips, 'Luckily, we're just Jas and Marko tonight.'

Marko kissed his way up to her ear. 'And Jas and Marko are in love.'

'Yes,' Jas said as she kissed him again. 'We most definitely are.'

EPILOGUE

Twelve months later, Kirribilli House, Sydney

'YOU'RE DOING IT AGAIN,' Marko murmured against Jas's ear.

Even now, after all this time, his proximity made her shiver.

Jas shrugged, and relaxed her bodyguard stance. She'd been scanning the crowd scattered across the perfect, sloping grass outside the Australian Prime Minister's Sydney residence: *faces and hands, faces and hands.* 'I can't help it,' she said. 'It's still part of me.'

Especially when she was so close to the Prime Minister—and, in the background, a few familiar faces from her old workplace. Four years ago, she'd worked here, at this spectacular one-hundred-and-fifty-year-old home with sweeping views across the water to the Opera House and the Sydney Harbour Bridge.

She'd been the one in the shadows, or on the

shoulders of members of Australian parliament or visiting dignitaries. Today, as wait staff in starched white shirts circulated with silver platters of canapés, *she* was one of those visiting dignitaries. As was Marko, of course, plus King Lukas, and Queen Petra—stunning, as always, in a raw silk dress and a tiara that caught every ray of the sun.

And Prince Filip. Aged nine months, on his first royal tour of Australia.

Fast asleep on the Dowager Queen's shoulder—Marko's mother was unable to face even a few weeks without her only grandchild— and with hair as golden as Petra's, Filip had no idea of the life ahead of him. The heir to the Vela Ada throne, born three months after King Lukas had returned to his rightful place in the palace—his treatment successful, his long-term prognosis excellent.

Unsurprisingly, Marko had not been upset that Filip had bumped him one place down the line of succession. Although he did worry for his tiny nephew. What if, like Marko, Filip was less than kingly?

Because, even now, Marko didn't exactly revel in his royal duties. The difference was that now he didn't pretend they didn't exist. Since Lukas has returned, Marko had still continued to attend the occasional royal engagement—in between his military commitments—to lessen the load on his still-recovering brother. The time Marko was spending at Vela Ada had also strengthened the relationship between the brothers, as Marko had finally torn down the playboy façade he'd been hiding behind for so long.

Jas had attended some of those royal engagements, too. In between her Gallagher Personal Protection Services commitments, of course. Although now she was—reluctantly—unable to work out in the field. A bodyguard who needed bodyguards of her own wasn't particularly useful.

Marko tugged on her hand, dragging Jas's attention away from a sleeping Filip.

'Want to go for a walk?' he asked.

'Can we do that?' Jas asked wistfully. The entire garden party mingled on the house side of a hedge that bordered the lawn. Beyond that the ground slid abruptly away to the harbour.

Marko shrugged. 'Speeches are done, why not?' Then he grinned. 'Besides, I'm a prince. Who's going to stop me?'

Well, potentially the Prime Minister's security detail—although, as they walked hand in hand beyond the hedges and to a stone-paved path that snaked between lush green gardens, no one halted their progress.

Eyes were trained on them, though. Strategically positioned amongst the gardens, at the perimeter, and even in bobbing boats on the harbour. Kirribilli House would be one of the most secure places in Australia, so this was hardly a private stroll.

The path eventually became steps, and those steps eventually made it to a jetty.

'Alone at last,' Jas said, with a grin, as they stood on the wide, wooden boards of the jetty.

'Not exactly,' Marko said, nodding towards the most visible guards out on the water.

Jas shrugged. 'Close enough.'

There were guaranteed to be some paparazzi out on the water too. Outside the exclusion zone, but close enough with a telephoto lens.

But it didn't matter.

Well, not enough for Jas to want to be anywhere else right now. Since they'd landed in Australia it had been a whirlwind. Here on this jetty, with Marko, it felt as if they finally had some space to breathe. If someone wanted to take a photo of that, then so be it.

It would only be a photo, after all.

A photo of Jasmine standing beside the man she loved.

Oh, she knew that a tabloid might splash a lurid headline on it—maybe *Prince Marko and his Aussie fiancée in harbourside tiff!* Or *Aussie Jasmine's shock declaration: set the date or it's over!*

It was ludicrous, the stories that could be written from the most benign photographs, but that was her life now. And, despite many, many shouty headlines, she and Marko were still very much in love. What the glossy magazines wrote had no bearing on their relationship. It didn't matter.

A photo couldn't hurt them. Heck, a naked selfie hadn't even been able to.

Because what they had was real and authentic—regardless of a photographer's lens, or a tabloid journalist's interpretation.

A breeze ruffled Jas's hair and pressed the silky fabric of her dress against her legs. Jas had been staring out towards the skyscrapers of the Sydney CBD, but she realised now that Marko was instead staring at her. She turned to face him.

'I've been thinking,' Marko said, very casually. But his grip on her hand was suddenly much firmer. 'About our engagement.'

Jas's smile was slow. 'Our fake engagement?'

'Yes,' he said, 'that one.' He paused. 'I wondered,' he continued, 'if you'd like to make it real.'

'Right now?' Jas said, grinning like an idiot, but also a bit surprised. 'Surrounded by security and photographers?'

'I'd planned to ask you back home, at our beach,' he said, but then he grinned wickedly. 'But then I kind of liked the idea of some paparazzo finally actually photographing something significant and real, and having no idea.'

'Plus we'll get photos of the moment,' Jas pointed out. 'About time we got something useful out of them.'

Marko took her other hand in his, so their fingers were perfectly laced together.

'Exactly,' he agreed. 'Although I'd really rather they were photographing a *yes*.'

Jas met Marko's gaze as he looked at her, losing herself, for the millionth time, in the silvery blue of his eyes.

'Yes,' she said softly. 'It's definitely a yes.'

Then Marko leant towards her, and whispered against her lips.

'*Dragi moj*, let's give them something worth photographing?'

Jas sighed against his mouth. 'Yes, please.'

Then they kissed.

And when they did, they weren't the playboy and the bodyguard, or even the Prince and his princess-to-be.

They were just Jas and Marko.

In love.

* * * * *

LET'S TALK
Romance

For exclusive extracts, competitions
and special offers, find us online:

 facebook.com/millsandboon

@millsandboonuk

@millsandboon

Or get in touch on 0844 844 1351*

For all the latest titles coming soon,
visit millsandboon.co.uk/nextmonth

*Calls cost 7p per minute plus your phone company's price per
minute access charge

Want even more
ROMANCE?

Join our bookclub today!

THE PRINCE'S
FAKE FIANCÉE